SHORTS FROM
HEREFORD AND WORCESTER

Edited by

SUZI BLAIR

NEW FICTION

First published in 1993 by
NEW FICTION
4 Hythegate, Werrington
Peterborough,
PE4 7ZP

Printed in Great Britain by Forward Press.

Foreword

The advent of New Fiction signifies the expansion of what has traditionally been, a limited platform for writers of short stories. New Fiction aims to promote new short stories to the widest possible audience.

The *Shorts* collections represent the wealth of new talent in writing, and provide enjoyable, interesting and readable stories appealing to a diversity of tastes.

Intriguing and entertaining; from sharp character sketches to 'slice of life' situations, the stories have been selected because each one is *a good read*.

This collection of short stories is from the pens of the people of Hereford and Worcester. They are new stories, sweeping across the spectrums of style and subject to reflect the richness of character intrinsic to the region, today.

Suzi Blair
Editor.

Contents

p. 60 missing

no page 142.

First Contact

by

Sean Jeffery

My first impression of this strange land in which I had found myself was of the thick and cloying atmosphere, unhealthy surely for the lungs of the inhabitants. My ship had landed in the cover of a small forest, its trees towering yet spindly, and only the colour of its foliage bearing any resemblance to those of our own world.

I clambered down the landing stage, and as it glided back into place I inhaled the stale air carefully. A pale white orb watched me from the velvet sky. A chill caressed my spine.

In the distance, I could see the lights of what must presumably be civilization. I could hear the drone of unfamiliar machinery. I composed myself and strode towards the sound. A wet mulch squelched beneath my feet in the semi-darkness. Had I the curiosity of a scientist I would have tested it, but since I had neither this nor the time to spare on this reconnaissance mission I did not. Instead, I continued my nerve-jangling journey until something tough and wiry crunched under my foot, and with a flapping of feathered wings some kind of wild creature squawked deafeningly in my face and rose swiftly, heading towards the woods. For a few moments I was frozen to the spot. In the coolness of the alien night, my vulnerability suddenly struck me. I breathed in deeply, and slowly began again.

I had been reassured that the people of this world were reasonably intelligent, and that contact would be quite straightforward.

This was an assumption made by intellectuals sitting in comfortable space observatories, picking up radio signals on huge receivers which had until now been answered only with the infinite silence of space. Those intellectuals were just twinkles in their fathers' eyes when the first man stepped on Mars. They could only try to imagine the exhilaration and the terror of that first explorer, and that of the first to face extra-terrestial life. No amount of reassurances or training could prepare me for that.

Thirty strides later, I halted again, sinking into the mulch. Cold sweat gripped my forehead like talons. A small, bright yellow eye was floating just within my field of vision, directly in front. There was a brief rustling as it moved closer and closer, and then it was just inches from my face, examining me. I had to put a hand across my face because of its intensity. I squinted, but saw nothing but piercing radiance. I felt a rush of air, a deep, throaty roar, and it was gone. I turned around quickly. The mulch almost sucked my shoes off. The eye, now red, was watching me again - perhaps the beast was enraged? - I half-turned, preparing to run as fast as I could; however, the beast must have been backing away, for the eye was getting smaller and smaller, and I could make out a hump and two horns - unless my eyesight was deceiving me - heading towards the woods, silhouetted in the eerie moonlight. My heart was beating at my chest as if desperate for escape.

After an uneventful further ten yards or so, I reached some sort of rectangular structure, made from a peculiarly soft wood. It rose high above me into the darkness. I could make out a fence, disappearing out of sight on both sides. Scrabbling in the dimness, I eventually found what could only be a handle, over-large though it seemed, and solid and unyielding. The fact that it was at head height made it more difficult to budge. Finally, it swung towards me, creaking ominously and almost knocking me off my feet. In spite of the gate's massive height, I had to enter the gap it left sideways. The creatures that inhabited this place must be indeed extraordinary.

On the other side, a hard, gritty substance greeted my tired feet. I took in my surroundings. On my left, a gargantuan wall loomed. Tipping my head backwards, I could see a sloped roof, outlined by artificial light. To my right was a similar construction, and ahead I could see more lights, flashing and darting about, only a two minute walk ahead. The sounds of machinery were much closer now.

I stood there, contemplating my next move. My breath rasped against my throat. I took a step forward, and immediately I was bathed in a pool of orange light. I looked about urgently for its source: it was up above me - a transparent sphere on top of a metal pole. I cursed as I ricked my neck examining it. Suddenly realizing that this might be some kind of security light, warning against intruders, I lunged towards the building to my left, straight into a small cluster of vegetation I had failed to notice. Thorns scratched my hands and face - I could almost feel alien viruses tingling as they entered my bloodstream.

I waited for ten minutes, which passed by painfully slowly, for I was eager now to get my mission over with. When there was no sign of movement nearby, I commenced once more towards the droning and the lights.

The pathway leading from the gate came to an end. My breathing was so loud now I am sure that it echoed. I was standing at the edge of a much wider thoroughfare. To the left and to the right, buildings even larger than the first two I had encountered soared into the heavens. These were different though, being decorated here and there with large square windows, multi-coloured and too brilliant for the eye. And at last I found the machinery: dark metal boxes with radiant eyes, propelled by rubber discs two or three at a time from two directions, cutting through the air inches from me like hellish messengers.

Below the roaring and whooshing of the machines, I could hear squawking and shrieking, and a lower cry very much like the sound of the horned beast near the forest. When there was eventually a gap between the metal boxes, icicles sprang from my backbone. I could see two strange beings, striding as if on stilts through the choking air. One of them turned towards me and let out that guttural noise as I stood there staring, fixed to the spot like a hunted animal.

There was an ethereal screech to my right, and I turned shakingly, only to face one of those stilt-like legs. I swallowed, and it was like swallowing thorns. I looked up, craning my neck, at the face of an alien. It looked down, perhaps as scared as me. It had twice as many eyes as we have - tiny, useless-looking slits with a pin-point of black. Oversized ovals of skin graced either side of its larger oval head, which pivoted on a reed-like protrusion from its angular, fragile trunk. Another growth of skin, a shapeless lump with one-too-many nostrils, bulged from the centre of its face, above two flaps of pinkish membrane. Its arms were rope-like, ending in wiry digits too numerous to contemplate.

I attempted to communicate with the being. All I received was a mixture of terror and bewilderment. Then it struck me how stupid I had been. Of course - they communicated with each other by sound - hence the shrieks and the roars.

They had not yet developed telepathy, the people of this planet, Earth.

A Hard Day's Work

by

David Phillips

Mature Cheddar. Terry's face clenched in a smile as he took another bite. Not a big deal, but another sign that things were getting better. Helen hated mature cheese. She preferred the mild stuff and insisted on buying it. During all those months he was out of work she maintained that every penny counted and she had to buy the cheapest. Now once more he had a job. They were gradually putting their life together again and this was another small sign. Without saying a word she had bought the cheese he preferred for his lunch box.

Terry leant back against the tree trunk. Helen had been hinting lately that they ought to go on holiday. She fancied Ibiza. A better class of people went there, rather than the Costa del Sol where they had been last time. Yes they must start thinking about a holiday. Two years without one had made the problems with their marriage much worse. Today would be a good day to be on holiday he thought to himself. The warmest day so far this year. Fresh leaves on the trees and clumps of flowers in the hedgerows. Life really was pleasant.

He would have liked to know more about flowers and birds and things. He had never taken much interest and couldn't tell one thing from another. Actually, this was quite a spot for such things. When the plans for the motorway had been announced there had been campaigns and demonstrations to stop it. This was one of the few places left where certain rare plants, birds, and even, he recalled, spiders still lived. He didn't pay much attention at the time, but he remembered that ordinary working folk, not just eggheads, had joined in the protest. Not just local people either. They had come from all over the country to fight the plan, but of course it hadn't made any difference. It never does. He looked around again. Yes, it was beautiful. He reached out and picked a flower only a foot or so from where he was sitting. A tiny little thing. Smaller than a penny across, yet when you looked carefully it really was superb. He wondered if it was one of the flowers all the fuss had been about.

He couldn't remember any names. It was all happening when their marriage was going through its worst phase. They hadn't been able to go out, to buy a drink, they had even had to cut down on fags. One of the worst arguments had been over who had smoked the last one in the packet. Helen had packed her

4

bags and got as far as the front door over that one. Looking back he could smile, particularly since Helen had given it up now; but it wasn't funny at the time. It's terrible what being out of work can do to people. He leant back against the tree trunk again and felt the warm sun on his face. Thank goodness he now had his job and everything was coming together again.

Behind him a bird called. He peered round the tree, but there was no bird to be seen. What he did see was horrible. A wide swathe of land had been turned into a desert. The top soil had been scraped away and pushed into a huge pile. Further over the trees and shrubs which had been removed were in another pile ready for burning, and stretching away into the distance was a wide river of clay. It was churned with the marks of bulldozer tracks and it was dead. What an ugly contrast with what remained on his side of the tree. And of course, this was the next bit to go. The flower he had just examined and the trees and hedgerows around would become a continuation of the desert behind him. He could see now why all those people had protested.

Helen hadn't been very sympathetic over the protesters. Watching the local television news one day she had made remarks about the women who had taken their young children with them to stand outside the council offices where the public enquiry had been held. It was pouring with rain and they all looked a sorry sight. 'Fancy putting the kids through that', she said, 'just for the sake of a few fields.' Of course that had led to more arguments. Everything led to arguments in those days. The fact was, Helen badly wanted a child, but they couldn't face the prospect of a family the way things were. Still, now he had a job, that was something else they could consider. He paused in his chewing. Was there more to the matter of his favourite cheese in the sandwiches than he knew? Did Helen know something she hadn't told him. He wouldn't mind; he would be pleased in fact, but remembering some of the things he had said in anger in past arguments he could well imagine she was hesitant to tell him now.

He would have to think of a few subtle questions to ask when he got home. The trouble was, being subtle wasn't one of his strengths. Perhaps a few pointed jokes would elicit the truth. He was good at jokes. Already he had convinced himself that Helen was pregnant and revelling in the thought. Yes, things really were looking better now. But, there was an afternoon's work ahead of him before going home to Helen. He flicked the dregs from the last cup of tea in his flask. Screwed the top back on and repacked his lunch box. He walked slowly across to his bulldozer. He heaved himself up to the driver's cab, settled himself into the seat and switched the huge beast into action. A few

5

more days and he would have finished the surface scrape ready for the main construction team to come in. He moved forward towards the tree where he had just been sitting. Oh yes, it was good to have a job again.

Re-union

by

Joyce Wilkinson

Kate followed the signs which directed her to the Parking place at the edge of the Playing Fields, parked her car, and walked up the drive to the School Entrance. It was familiar and yet strange, smaller than she had remembered, but after all, fifty years had passed since she had been inside. There had been reunions; she had never bothered to attend. 'Why now?' she asked herself, although in her heart she knew the answer. Perhaps Vicki and James would be there. She hoped and feared that they might be. The paragraph in the newspaper had been brief but explicit. The school was closing down, making room for luxury flats for the elderly, and today had been declared an Open Day. Any ex-pupils had been invited to pay a final nostalgic visit to the old building.

A very confident and modern-looking sixth-former (no flat heels and gymslips now) ushered her in and asked if she wanted a guided tour. With a somewhat condescending smile, Kate declined the offer, and directed her steps to the Assembly Hall. There were a few people inside, idly looking at the Sports' Trophies, and the portraits on the walls. A quick glance at the visitors convinced Kate that she did not know any of them. Nothing seemed to have changed; the rows of hard forms filled the body of the Hall. It was easy to recall the whispered conversations between the girls, while the Headmistress, in her exalted position on the platform, lifted her voice in seemingly endless morning prayers.

With surprising clarity, Kate remembered the actual words in which she and Vicki had discussed the signs of the Zodiac on one such morning.

'My sign is Taurus - the Bull,' said Vicki.

'That's obvious,' hissed a spiteful voice on the left, while Kate, on the right, hurried to cover up the cruel comment. They all knew that it had been an allusion to Vicki's nose, her wide nostrils and thick lips.

'Well, I'm a Libran - they love beauty, you know.'

She dropped her head, conscious that she had made things worse for Vicki. It was the last thing she wished to do, because Vicki was her friend. Still, it had been poor Vicki who had been hauled up in front of the Assembly and reprimanded for talking, and at the recollection, Kate felt a new wave of pity for her, and it seemed to her that this trifling incident so long ago, epitomised their lives. She was a true Libran, beautiful, artistic and clever, whereas Vicki showed none of the characteristics of her Taurus birth sign. There was nothing 'bullish' or aggressive in her make-up. She was just ordinary, solid and reliable, and a good friend who was always there, drawn to Kate, like a moth to a brilliant flame.

It was not surprising that both the girls had fallen in love with James; he was so kind, so charming, and so handsome. Everyone decided that he and Kate made a perfect pair. They thought so too, and began to make plans for their wedding, sure that the future would be wonderful. They gave no thought to the inescapable fact that one can never be sure of the future. When, on a short business trip, James was injured and terribly burned in an air crash, Kate felt that her whole world had ended.

She was still an attractive woman, but even all the careful and expensive cherishing of her once outstanding beauty had not been able to hold back the wrinkles which had appeared through the passing of the many years. The label, 'elderly' could now truthfully be applied to her. How she hated that word - how she hated anything drab and ugly! Even so, she was aware that there was admiration in some of the glances that followed her as she made her way from the Hall, to the Gymnasium where light refreshments were being served. There were quite a lot of people seated at the small tables, and she looked in vain for a familiar face. Not finding one, she sat down at an empty table in the corner, idly wondering what had happened to the heavy, long refectory tables on which the school meals used to be served. She wanted to talk to somebody, anybody, but she couldn't, not even to the school-girl who quietly placed a cup of tea and some biscuits in front of her. All that she could manage was a somewhat abrupt 'Thank you.' What else was there to say? Today's schoolgirls had little in common with her contemporaries - and where were they now?

Kate found herself staring unashamedly into the faces of the people around her; one or two stared back, some even smiled. Try as she might to effect a transformation, the faces remained those of strangers. She turned her attention to another group. They were sitting at tables half-hidden by a stack of spare chairs, but Kate had excellent long vision. By looking intently at each face, she could make out the features of most of the men and women there.

As if feeling the strength of the searching stare, one woman with her back to Kate, wheeled round and looked straight at her. In that moment Kate saw the face of the man who was opposite to her. She gasped in instant revulsion as she realised that the mask-like expressionless features created by a skilful plastic surgeon, belonged to James. As she had done before, she shuddered and turned back to look at the woman. She would have recognised that nose anywhere. It had not been changed, and yet, she looked almost beautiful. There was a kind of radiance surrounding her.

How awful to have spent all those years, constantly looking at such a travesty of beauty! Kate indulged in a comforting kind of pity for Vicki, although she wore no expression of misery - and no sign of recognition on her face either. Had she herself then changed so much? Was her beauty so much less durable than that of the exquisite treasures with which she had surrounded herself in her life of success and wealth? Vicki, she was sure, would never intentionally ignore anyone. After all, it had been a very long time. Perhaps it was just a trick of the light, and possibly Vicki's sight was not as sharp as hers. Why not go over and speak to them? It was meant to be a re-union, and there would be so much to talk about. She would tell them that although she had gone away and not kept in touch, she had never forgotten them.

Surely they would be interested in the wonderful places she had seen on her travels. She could describe the fabulous Eastern palaces, the blue seas, the sunsets and the tropical islands, the brilliance of the birds' plumage, and the intoxicating perfume of the flowers. She could tell them all this, but she could not tell James that although she had been loved by many men, she had never forgotten him, and had never married. In her remembering however, he was always as he had been at their first meeting.

She hesitated, absorbed in her memories, while the buzz of conversation went on around her. When she next glanced in the direction of James and Vicki, they had risen to their feet, obviously preparing to leave. Unless she moved forward now to speak to them, she would lose them again. She put down her half empty cup and took one step in their direction, only to stop dead, frozen to the spot, as she saw the figure of a man framed in the doorway. Even at that distance she could see his features quite clearly. She felt her heart hammering in her chest as she looked at the handsome face, the illuminating smile. For a breathless moment she thought that he was coming to her. It was hard to resist the impulse to hold out her arms to him, but instead he embraced Vicki and gripped his father's hand.

Kate heard him say, 'It's raining a little, but I've brought the car up to the front entrance, Mother.'

They went out together and were gone from sight, but Kate remained staring vacantly into space.

'Are you all right?' asked a voice at her elbow.

9

Kate pulled herself together and turned to the girl who was collecting empty teacups.

'Yes, oh yes. I'm fine thank you. I was just leaving.'

With a rueful smile she picked up her bag, and walked steadily to the door. There would be no re-union now. She had been unable to pay the price that love had asked, and had pitied Vicki, who had done so. But Vicki did not need her pity, now or then. For the first time she realised that Beauty too, had to be paid for, and she knew that the price which she had paid had been too high.

Mushrooms

by

Ronald Hutton

During late Autumn, in the natural cycle of events, this deliciously edible fungi is in waning season, but still used for prime dish garnishing; or eaten as the main dish ingredient with thick gravy covering gammon rather and fried potato fritters. Some mushroom lovers prefer firm young 'buttons' whilst others lean toward a leavening of older stools enriching the dish with a gamy tang.

Many years ago, as a young boy looking through wonder-filled eyes at a universe bounded by grass meadows and green hills, where water courses played host to their courtier flora and fauna, my father would take my hand and together we would explore the misty world of Autumn's early mornings. There we beheld the ephemeral kingdom of the mushrooms!

They started up before the eyes, like gnome umbrellas, the white domes thrusting to keep at bay the silver dewed spangles of spider webs covering the rough grass with delicate tracery. Those of earlier birth surviving the eager hands of human gatherers remained only to give life to a myriad of grubs before their own inevitable and final decay. Thus I was privileged at early age to stand on the threshold of universal understanding. There was magic in the world for a small boy, and a strong father stood at his side.

Two decades later, walking alone down the paths of yester-year where once we had walked together, still burning with impotent anger at fate that intervened as the child emerged to manhood and took one away forever, the memories of those early mushroom expeditions came flooding back; but the child of yesterday had advanced no further over the threshold of universal understanding - today's uniformed executioner was sobbing his great grief at the loss of a father.

Upon my return, from hills and jungle, I observed the fields no longer gave forth their bountiful harvest of mushrooms. Opinions vented in the welcoming fug of the village public house were sometimes funny, sometimes furious, but always diverse.

'It's the artificial fertilizers - bloody muck if you ask me,' observed one pint-sipper, with totally unconscious humour.

'No horses any more,' opined another. 'All bloody tractors and diesel fumes'.

'D'you remember,' reminisced a third, 'that time when the farmer was up waiting for us by that field he grew 'em in - and Bill ripped the arse out of his trousers jumping that barbed wire fence to get away?'

'Ahh!' confirmed Bill. 'It was a bloody dear breakfast that time.'

'My bloody breakfast - you left yours behind,' observed another with sour recollection.

So with the blunt good humour of their kind men of childhood acquaintance sought to help wash away the angry pus, of my first hot grief, to start the healing process that time alone would allow.

Later in life, I remember my unit being encamped on the rugged coastline of Pembrokeshire, and the unofficial intelligence network of the regiment (the advance party) had worked overtime in preparing a 'sitrep' for the main body's arrival. Additional to the usual information relating to the availability of hostelries and female company (the descriptive vernacular of the British Army inhibits publication of such in minutia), a wealth of mushrooms had been discovered in a fold of ground hidden from the camp by a low profiled ridge.

Bonanza!

For the first time in the battalion's history, covies of soldiers broke the cover of their tents an hour before the bugle sent its compulsive notes ringing through the thin morning air. Several brace of subalterns could often be seen mushrooming as avidly as their men. Even an occasional field-rank was observed, taciturn and unapproachable, making a lonely peripheral picking.

One man face a major crisis - his seasonal and heightened love affair with mushrooms conflicted with his continuing and stable relationship with his early morning bed.

He was the 'Q' bloke, treated with reverence by Commanding Officer and latrine wallah alike. I have demurred with my Brigadier, but never with the lowliest Quartermaster. If ingratiated sufficiently with this holy man, a mug of cook's tea would be yours under the heaviest mortar stonk; incur his displeasure and rations would always be at a premium!

The first morning he arrived in Mess and saw those deliciously steaming mushrooms cooked for smug faced pickers, he attempted to acquire some by appealing to the generosity of breakfast neighbours. The refusals were short, sharp and pithy, in the time honoured vocabulary of the British Army!

After two morning of unhesitating rebuffs, the 'Q' retired to rethink tactics. On the third morning he strode early into breakfast, with chairs still sparsely taken, and rubbed his hands in histrionic anticipation.

'Right,' he roared to the deferent waiter, 'Let's have my mushrooms, then, with the usual.'

'Sir.' The waiter scurried away and shortly returned with the breakfast plates. Reposing in full glory were the prized mushrooms.

'Hello there,' said a late arrival. 'Mushrooms eh? Didn't see you picking this morning.'

'That's because you were too bloody late getting up,' replied the 'Q. 'Can't understand what you blokes see in staying in bed that long!'

Every morning for the rest of the stay at that camp, 'Q' would unhurriedly arise, stroll into breakfast, and demand his mushrooms; occasionally, for good measure, he would ask where the rest were, and tuck into a feast he certainly had not personally garnered.

Returning from camp, he found himself in a train compartment with men whose talk eventually fastened on mushrooms.

'I certainly had far fewer for breakfast than I picked,' grumbled one.

Without exception, the rest concurred. 'It's those bloody cooks - they'll pinch anything,' was the general verdict.

'Q' exchanged glances with me - in the depths of his grey eyes, I swear I observed the faintest glimmer of a smile...

A Life Among Old Books

by

E R Slade

Uncle ran a second-hand bookshop full of dreary tomes that had collected the dust of ages; they were as dead as the poor men who had spent hour upon hour writing them, imagining, no doubt, that they were giving birth to a masterpiece, that they were carving out for themselves, a small chunk of immortality, so that somewhere they would live on after their bodies had turned to dust.

Well, here they lived in rows, shelf upon shelf and sometimes in little piles upon the floor. Next to a set of four volumes on Lloyd George, lay a book entitled 'Pearl's Escape' and next to that a book with the curious title 'An Englishman looks at Wales'.

Uncle always wore a nondescript dark suit and must have been seventy - give or take a year or so. It is probable that he considered himself to be a man of the professions, on a par with a doctor or dentist, certainly on a higher rung of the ladder than book-maker or undertaker. Was he not providing a useful service? The students from the local university, hard up after they had spent much of their grants on beer, food and girl friends were apt to pop into the shop called 'Rudolph's' for cheap copies of the 'Plays of Shakespeare' or 'Byron's Poetical Works'.

Uncle breezed about the three of four rambling rooms, disappearing often into his inner office, into the 'inner sanctum' where the rare books were housed, safe from the prying eyes of the average customer. This little office, not much larger than a cubicle, bore a printed notice which said 'No admittance, Private'.

Uncle's main assistant was his nephew, a shortish man of about thirty years of age who had a look that could only be described as solemn. Just as a museum guide sitting hour after hour in a room full of statues, would find it hard to laugh, so Nephew, who spent his days among authors who meant little or nothing to him, could not be expected to find much humour in his situation. His occupation was somewhat similar to that of an undertaker, but if one gave thought to the matter, inferior to the undertaker; the undertaker saw promptly to the disposal of earthly remains and submitted his account. Nephew's job was not so easy. The remains left behind by literary men were not easy to clear up; there was evidence of this all around, row upon row, shelf upon shelf, room after room. In a grocer's shop, a packet of butter had a short life span; if not sold, it had to be dumped after a few weeks. Not so with the books; some had been in the shop when Nephew started out on his career of book selling, and he could see little hope of anybody buying them now. And yet, if someone came in, looking for a book entitled 'Pearl's Escape', he would answer in his slow, funereal voice: 'Yes, I think you are lucky, we do have a copy, let me get it for you'.

Uncle at seventy, seemed more content and at ease than his nephew, more ready with comments upon the weather or humorous quips to his customers. Nephew viewed the years ahead with little enthusiasm, countless years during which he stood patiently by the cash-till, waiting to sell books with titles such as 'How to Detect Fake Antiques', 'What Bird is That?' or 'Last Term at St Hilary's'. Uncle was a figure of some prominence in the city, he was moreover a free-mason and hob-nobbed with the dignitaries although they rarely came into his shop; they recommended him strongly if acquaintances died leaving for disposal a collection of books. It was on such occasions that the old man came into his own, getting often for a song, someone's once prized possessions. Nephew in his dust-coat was even seen to smile at the appearance of a fresh lot of books to grace the shelves, to replace 'How to detect Fake Antiques' and those that the hard-pressed students had snapped up in order to meet the deadline for their essays.

It was assumed by those who knew the shop that the owner would quietly fade away from the scene, take some years left to him in retirement and that his nephew would take over, helped by the girl who came in as a relief. Uncle's closest relative was now his nephew, and the younger man who had been there for ten years, deserved some recognition for his perseverance.

It came as more than a mild shock when there appeared in the front window of the shop one morning a handwritten notice stating 'Business and Stock for Sale'. It was rumoured by some that uncle and nephew had quarrelled, although it was difficult to imagine the younger man raising his voice in anger about anything. Others said that the nephew had lost patience with the dusty books and wanted to go abroad. Two or three laughed, wondering who on earth would want to take on and pay good money for rooms full of dusty and largely unsaleable books.

There were few serious enquiries for the lease and stock; a bookseller from a town nearby made an offer which was considered ridiculous; he explained the low figure when he said that most of the books were of no use to him and would have to be thrown out. He spoke the truth but the truth often hurts. Uncle was so upset, that he took two whole days' leave of absence.

Eventually an offer came which was accepted. The likely buyer was new to book selling, but clearly had money since he had come from London to Wales and had bought an expensive house on the coast. It was, as he said, a lifelong ambition of his to run a bookshop. With his wife, he went from room to room looking at the rows of books he would shortly take over. It was arranged that Nephew would stay on for a while to show then the ropes as they were new to the world of second-hand book selling.

Then for some reason, the deal fell through; the couple had second thoughts and backed away. Possibly, in the cold light of reason, the sight of all those books depressed them. Three days later, the owner collapsed in his office among a pile of 'rare' books and did not recover.

Nephew thus became sole owner of the rambling shop and its contents. The shop closed for three days 'owing to family bereavement'. Uncle received a written tribute in the evening paper under the heading 'Well-known local book-seller dies'. The 'For Sale' notice was removed from the shop window.

The new owner was interviewed briefly and photographed for a short article in the evening paper. It is hardly surprising that the journalist found him taci-turn. It was reported that he intended to continue running the shop as his uncle had done; there would be no immediate changes. The girl who helped on Satur-days came on a regular basis, three days a week. One noticeable difference was that the dust coat was hung permanently on a hook in the inner office. The new owner had taken to wearing a dark suit now that he had become a 'professional' man. Malicious tongues said it was the one worn by his uncle; if so, it must have been altered by a tailor since the two men were not of the same size. The expression on the new owner's face did not change from when he had been the assistant; it was the same long suffering expression as always. But now that he was in charge, he could say 'The shop is closing now' and close a few minutes early if he wanted to do so.

The End of the Journey

by

Margaret Crew-Smith

The train was delayed at Richmond and so it pulled into Waterloo half an hour late. The morning workers were out in force, this he hated as since the war he kept away from crowds as much as possible.

Pushing through the crush he made his way down the stairs towards the buses, the queue was already long and his heart sank. If he could only get a seat on Red Arrow 502 he would be alright, but too many passengers were already on board, and he had to stand.

If the bus started straight away he might feel better, he moved to one side and holding on to the rail across the window pressed his aching head against the cool glass and closed his eyes. There was some trouble with the coin machine, he heard someone rattling it to get their money back, that meant a delay while the driver cleared the fault, then a sudden surge of people pressing around him, a sharp jerk as the bus eased forward and the journey began.

The pain in his head remained, he smelt garlic on someone's breath, and the fear assailed him, was he back with all the other Jews aboard a truck that was only meant for cattle, and to the Germans his race were nothing more than that.

Almost afraid now to open his eyes for his senses were confused, he was conscious of a slowing down and halting of the vehicle. People moved as the exit doors opened and a few passengers alighted. He forced himself to look and saw the comfortable restaurant already filling with customers, then the doors of the bus closed and they were on the move again.

If I stay calm, he thought, I shall be alright, try thinking of safe every day things. This has caught me out before, last time it was the close packed lift at Gloucester Road but then I was worse because I ended up screaming like a mad man and they carted me off to hospital. The doctor had understood though, apparently his father had helped liberate one of the camps after the war, the memory of the poor wretches unable to crawl let alone walk had never left him.

The bus was less full now but still all seats were taken. Windscreen wipers were noisily clearing away the rain which had suddenly descended, his window was misted and using his sleeve he cleaned a patch to see through. They had stopped for traffic lights, a small church stood on a patch of grass, he knew the church, he knew where he was, he was safe, he was back with his family, he was going to the office and it was a normal day, but the badge of the RAF on the wooden notice board threw him completely off his guard.

To him, looking at it, knowing it for what it was yet some sick thing inside him took over and placed upon the board, the German eagle, and set in motion the waking nightmare which he dreaded.

The same indifferent faces looked at the passengers from the pavement, no help could be expected there. The vehicle stopped and more men and women were herded on, a uniformed figure roughly told them to make room for more, he waited for the expected blow to fall on those who were not quick enough to move, and was surprised when nothing happened.

Perhaps it's alright after all, he thought, maybe I am just being silly, but wait a minute, that's what I thought before, and look what happened, there was this camp, even then I thought it might be alright. The doctor was kind, he let me help him, I told him how sick Jacob my brother was, and he said to bring him down, and I did, then I found what they really did to sick Jews. I tried to kill myself after Jacob was left to die in agony, but they saved me just to have the pleasure of seeing me suffer. I should have died eventually, but soldiers in khaki uniforms arrived and then I was in hospital, but after that I don't remember, I don't remember, except a nurse who cried and I could feel her tears upon my face, and thought to see an angel weep can only happen to a very few.

A Haunting We Will Go

by

John Mayall

It is a sad comment on our social system when you find yourself employed as a Security Guard on a little old church and its spooky cyprus-covered church-yard.

Only last week they broke into the vestry, drank all the communion wine, nicked a gold chalice and the Sunday collection, and then went out into the churchyard and brutally emasculated all the previously well-endowed cherubs on the late Mayor's very expensive memorial.

'We can't have this happening then, can we, Hobbs?' my boss said to me. 'So your stint for tonight is the cemetery patrol, so to speak. Keep an eye on everything and don't be frightened, eh!' We both laughed.

It was a damp night with an icy wind making the cyprus branches creak and cast weird, restless, shadows to dance around the tombstones in the eerie light of the full Hallowe'en moon.

I went once around the outside of the church, marching rhythmically to keep the cold out. Soon the rhythm had me chanting quietly:-

> Ho, ho, Hallowe'en,
> Soon the Witches will be seen,
> Some in black and some in green,
> Ho, ho, Hallowe'en!

A sudden movement in front brought me to a halt. A shadow? Two bright yellow eyes stared up at me, reflecting the moon, and a cat stood, rigid, in my path with its hair standing on end all over it. I carried on with my march and, with a spitting squeal, it disappeared amongst the long grass between the graves.

The church seemed secure enough and so I rested in the shelter of the porch for a nice long while, safe and out of the wind.

After a time conscience began to whisper the words of the boss to me.

'Your stint for tonight is the Cemetery Patrol.' So, unwelcoming though it was, I thought I'd better get out there amongst those mossy tombstones.

19

The late Mayor's grave was most impressive, and I was glad to see that the stone mason had made a good job of restoring each one of the cherub's damaged esteems even more generously than before. I hoped it wouldn't invite yet another wave of vandalism.

It was then that I read the scroll that the rather butch cherubs were holding:

'From ghosties and ghoulies
And long-leggity beasties
And things that go bump in the night
Good Lord deliver us.'

Something went bump! And then it went bump again!

It was coming from the church porch where I had been sheltering only a minute ago. With the lack of speed of an old time British Bobby I strolled back with disarming indifference.

One of the outside doors of the porch, which had been left open, had swung shut. The moon at that moment was obscured by a passing cloud and I could see only inky blackness in that porch.

Using all my professional training I stood still and listened. Nothing. Alert to anything I stepped into the blackness. Just then the moon came out again and revealed that the securing bolt on the door had slipped. So it was the wind which had caught it.

Thankful of the shelter I again lingered in the porch watching a multitude of cloud shadows speeding up the hill to the church, like some large Victorian family late for Sunday service.

But there was something strange about two of those shadows. They were a bit more fitful, a bit more furtive, than the others. They were something other than just cloud shadows. Figures, perhaps of people, but definitely moving figures.

Again my professional training provided the reflex action and I stepped back into the shadows to watch.

They were hooded, like monks, and I had a cold, uneasy feeling come upon me.

As they drew closer I saw they each clutched a heavy crowbar in their right hands, and were wearing old rain-soaked anoraks.

They made straight for the late Mayor's flamboyant memorial and, as they reached it, they raised their crowbars over their heads.

'The cherub neuterers!' I thought as I moved out of the porch and into a shaft of moonlight to confront them.

Just as they looked up, I clutched the front folds of my shroud and opened it with outstretched arms.

Two crowbars fell from fearful hands and, as the figures turned and ran stumbling down the hill, the silence of the night was shattered by panicking voices begging for mercy.

Visiting Grandma

by

Jessica Jones

The passengers exchanged horrified glances as the plane nosedived. The Captain advised them to fasten their seat belts while he and his co-pilot dealt with a 'technical problem'.

The man sitting behind Harriet began complaining about the amount of money he'd spent recently to overcome his fear of flying.

Everyone breathed a sigh of relief when the plane levelled up again. It seemed a bit late for the stewards to repeat the safety demonstration they'd given at the beginning of the flight, but they did it anyway. Only moments afterwards the hum of the engines stopped and the plane started falling.

The man behind Harriet shouted, 'Oh God, I knew it. I always knew it. If I ever take a plane,' I used to tell people, 'I'll be the one that doesn't make it.'

The Captain told them all to find and study the card illustrating the escape procedure. Harriet felt sick. She obeyed mechanically. She fumbled with the card hidden in the deep pocket of the chair-back in front of her. Stiff with fright she pulled it out. She didn't want to look at it. She didn't want to think about struggling with the handle on the emergency exit door, or sliding down the inflatable chute to the ground.

A priest called out to anyone who thought they could find a mustard seed of faith to silently join him in prayer, that each and every one should be delivered safely to their intended destination.

A woman started screaming. Somebody slapped her hard and her cries became muffled. Husbands and wives, lovers, parents and children took each others hands and held them firmly. Those travelling alone gripped their arm rests.

'I sure wish I was some place else,' said the girl in the seat next to Harriet.

'I know what you mean,' Harriet replied. 'Got anywhere particular in mind?'

'Oh, any place, dear God, any place but here.' And then, after a pause she added, 'My parents' farm - I guess that's where I should be - apologising for all the mean things I said at the weekend. I lost my temper. They've never accepted me going off to live in the big city. They never wanted me to be a jet-setting business woman. They wanted me to stay in the country and settle down with some local boy. Believe me, at this precise moment I wish I had done. How about you? Are you thinking about all the things you might not get to say to your family?'

'No,' said Harriet, 'My family are all dead.'

'How about a boyfriend then? I bet you have a boyfriend.'

'We split up a few months ago when I discovered he was a rat. There's nothing I would want to say to him. But I do have a favourite place. Well, it doesn't really exist anymore unless I shut my eyes and imagine it. If I could be anywhere else now I'd go and visit Grandma. Her house was where I loved to be as a child. During the difficult growing up years after she'd died, I'd pretend I was back there whenever I got lonely or scared.

Grandma's place was so inviting. On Sunday mornings in winter, the smell of roast beef would seep out through every crack. We usually arrived just before lunch. When Grandma opened the door to greet us, instead of drowning us, the smell would vanish for the next few minutes while she squeezed us to her enormous body. Nothing could get up your nose during one of those hugs, not even air.

Grandma's house was like her. The chairs were soft and comfortable, and so large you could snuggle down in them and almost disappear.

The fruit trees in her garden were like her too. The rosy faced apples were huge. The pears were wide-hipped and the plums as plump as could be. And there was always a bumper crop - plenty to give away to family and friends and plenty to turn into jam. She even used to leave a basket full by the gate for the scrumpers. I don't know how things grew so well in that garden; it never seemed to rain there.'

The plane appeared to be falling faster now. Harriet turned to look at her fellow traveller. The girl's eyes were closed. Perhaps she was dreaming of home. Harriet shut her eyes. She sat in the generous shade of one of Grandma's apple trees munching salad. Grandma swatted a fly away from the lemonade. Fat bees bumbled around the fruit which dangled from the branches overhead. The rhythmic thud of tennis balls on nearby courts echoed in the stillness of the late summer afternoon.

Harriet was shaken out of her daydream by a juddering sensation. The Captain was speaking to them, but she couldn't make out what he was saying. His voice was distorted. The girl beside her was folding a piece of paper which she waved at Harriet.

'If you get out of this alive and I don't, would you see this gets to my folks?'

'Of course,' Harriet replied.

23

'Thanks. Anything I can do for...'

There was a terrific bump. It threw Harriet right out of her seat. She didn't dare open her eyes at first, but she'd landed against something soft and she felt quite comfortable. She wasn't aware of any pain of any kind, although she was finding it difficult to breathe so she forced her eyes open.

Grandma relaxed her grip on Harriet and moved back a little to get a better look at her. Then she smiled the same round faced cheery smile that she always smiled.

Christmas Shopping

by

W Owens

'Sodding weather. Will it never stop?' he thought out loud, smudging the condensation from the windows with his anorak sleeve.

Mike Williams flicked the wipers which squeegeed across the screen. The droplets disappeared and they could follow, fading into the mist, the silhouette of Thomas.

'Think he'll be long?'

'Um, not too long, not in this weather.' Andrew looked at his watch. 'Back in time for us to get a few presents in Aber and have a pint or two before we have to get back home.' He reached across to the stereo and flicked it on. It was 'Police.' 'Every breath you take; every move you make, I'll be watching you.'

Outside the whole world had concertinered into a snarling, spitting vortex of wind and sleet that chilled deeper than the bone. The reed grass was smashed flat against the singing fence wire while the sleet drenched Thomas, sticking his shirt to his skin with wetness. Snow, like pieces of dandruff, speckled his face. It seemed that the whole world might die of cold, shivering into nothingness, like the pathetic flowers grasped in his hand, diminishing with each step, petals battered and blown away by the swirling wind.

Each Saturday of the long winter had been the same. Up at six, meet at the bus stop outside the Lloyds Bank in St Johns at six-thirty and then the long drive to Hereford, Abergavenny and then, finally, on to the cemetery in Brynmawr but it had never been like this before: never as wet and cold as this and they were all wrong. His grief hadn't eased. It will, they had said, but they didn't know anything about it: it had intensified, calcifying into a hurt which he carried around inside him like a cancer, from the first moment he had known.

It had been a Thursday, some time after two. He had been teaching Wordsworth to the Lower six, Alex dissecting Wordsworth's lyricism.

'It's all very well saying that about him but he didn't really know anything about it, did he, if he was a pantheist?' Then the phone had rung, summoning him to the office immediately. They hardly noticed him go, Alex vehemently dismissing 'The Daffodils' as romantic drivel, while he had walked the strangely quiet and long, polished corridor to Jenny's office, unease and uncertainty rising in his stomach. He knew as soon as he opened the door: Jenny was in tears, and there was a policewoman with her.

'I'm sorry Thom... it's Sue,' was all she could manage. Strange now, when he looked back, how he was able to remember the conversation, word for word, as he battled over the grass mounded coffins of the dead. In places the snow was deep enough to deceive and he left large, gaping footholes; in other places he stumbled awkwardly while memories jostled in his head for some sort of order. He remembered the WPC touching his arm; details of the pile-up; coffee rings staining the table.

None of them felt warm until they got back to the outskirts of Worcester but it had stopped snowing, Rushwick Christmas card pretty.

'So, do you fancy a pint or what Mike?'

'Sure. Thom hasn't got anything to go home for, has he? How about a Guinness? We could have a quick game of arrows in the Lamb and Flag?'

'Yeah, if you're paying -'

'Christ!' Suddenly, the steering wheel became alive as Mike spun the wheel to the right and hit the brakes, the car spinning and hissing on the snow as it slewed just out of reach of a lorry that had hurried out of a junction too slowly.

'The stupid sod!' Mike shouted at the window, adrenalin like a fire in his belly. It woke Thom up and disorientated him for a moment because he thought he'd been awake. 'That was a close one, Thom.'

'Was it? I missed it.'

The pub was packed, raucous laughter and cigarette smoke filling the air. His brothers sorted their way to the bar and then escaped with their pints and whiskey chasers. Thomas threw first. Double twenty and a seven.

'I am grateful to you lads, for coming down with me. You know that, don't you?'

'Shut up Thom. We loved Sue as much as you did. No one could have wished for a better sister-in-law.'

'Besides, what else would we be doing on a Saturday so close to Christmas? More bloody shopping for God's sake. That's the last time I go shopping in Abergavenny two weeks before Christmas. Hey, look at that.' Andrew pointed at the board. 'Double twenty and a treble nineteen.

'I don't know about you two but I can't get warm.' Mike downed his whiskey, a sliver running down his beard, and thumped it onto the table. He blew into his hands and rubbed them together as if he were washing them. 'I need a brandy. I'll get them in. Retrieve the darts for me Thom.'

Thomas moved too quickly. It was the whiskey he guessed, on an empty stomach. He reached to the board too quickly, Andrew's last dart catching him in the back of his hand, pinning it to the board. A woman, sitting by him, gasped, as it pierced his hand, pinning it to the board. Then she screamed. It was only when he didn't yell out, because he felt no pain, that he realised that there was something really wrong. Mike extracted it as quickly as he could but Thomas felt so cold, so stiff. So really sick. He needed to sit down. It was the shock. If he could just sit down for a minute he would be all right.

'I'm sorry Mike. That was stupid. I just don't feel too good. Let me sit down for a minute.' Someone had wrapped a handkerchief around his hand but there was no blood. Someone else shouted that there was a doctor in the lounge but Thomas was focussing on the table and the beer stains, beer mats, beer glasses, anything to help him fight off being sick. He felt so tired. He just needed to shut his eyes for a moment in order to stop the world spinning. It was then, he supposed, that he must have fallen asleep.

The snow was thick as ever, the flashing strobes painting it a kaleidoscope of blue. 'Poor bastards. They didn't stand a chance.'

'How many serge?'

'Three by the look of it but we can't get them out. We'll have to wait for the cutting crew. What a mess. Look at that one.' The sergeant nodded towards the back. There were Christmas presents scattered around the wreckage, blood-splattered paper and cellophane mixed with glass and debris. The man in the back had taken the worst of it. He was sprawled over, his head crushed, his arm twisted up against the back of the driver's seat. But the strangest thing was his hand. It was pinned against the seat by a shard of metal that looked remarkably like a dart.

Day Off

by

Ben Davies

She looked as though she had got out cf bed hurriedly and dressed impatiently. As she stooped in front of the kitchen range coaxing the kettle, she pushed her unruly hair from her eyes without noticing that her hand was grimy.

A ray of weak morning sunshine came through the cottage window, but it caught no light in her hair, which remained as dull as the unpolished range.

She turned her head expectantly at footsteps above, and breathed sharply through her nose as she watched where the staircase twisted into the living-room.

Tom came slowly and heavily into the kitchen in his pit clothes.

She frowned at the dull meekness of her husband's face, and turned back to the fireplace, resting her bare arm on the stretched wire that held a collection of unwashed clothes.

He stood there sensing the sullen anger of her stiff back, but though her foot tapped quickly on the fender he missed the warning and sighed and sat down at the table.

Instantly she swung round, eyes bright with temper: 'So, you're going after all?' she shrilled.

He nodded, and cut himself a slice of bread, 'We had enough of that last night. Don't let us have it over again, Rona.'

She banged the kettle from the fire, and laughed coldly, 'Don't stir things up!' she mimicked, 'scared of a row; scared of missing a shift; scared of everything, you are!'

Tom broke and munched his bread quietly, aggravating her.

'A nice fool I'll look,' she said, her voice rising, 'Going on my own to my brother's wedding.' She took a few steps towards the table, swaying in front of him, trying to catch his eye. But he went on eating with his eyes lowered.

'Where's Tom? they'll say,' and there was glitter in her eyes, 'Pity you had to come alone. And they'll look sort of sympathetic, and yet be full of glee like a lot of hissing snakes.'

'Look, I'm sick of this,' he said, 'I told you last night I wasn't going. I can't dodge a shift, and anyway we can't afford it. You'll get him married alright without me.'

'It's the look of it; they'll all be pitying me.'

'Pitying yourself more like,' he muttered, and took his jacket from the back of the chair and began to put it on.

'You ... you ...!' hissed Rona, and suddenly she was round the table and her grimy hand had slapped its black imprint on his face.

With his arms caught in the jacket he stood still, looking down at her with quiet contempt. He smiled a little: 'Make your brother think a bit if he saw us now!' he said.

Rona leaned back against the table, her face white and vicious. 'Go on - jeer!' she said, 'but you daren't take a shift off, even if it was for his funeral.'

He picked up his cap and went to the door. 'I suppose,' he said slowly, 'the pit ought to close for the day every time there's anything doing in your family.'

But she was not listening. She sank on to a chair, and with her elbows on the table and her fists pressed hard into her cheeks, she started to cry.

Tom smiled wryly and opened the door. She looked up at him, her face twisted and bitter: 'Go on - get out!' she shrieked, 'You musn't be late. Be like the rest of the sheep. But you haven't the guts of one of them even!'

Her voice rose hysterically, and Tom came back into the room and closed the door behind him.

'Oh, what's the use,' he growled, tossing his cap on to the table, 'This'll go on for weeks; breakfast and night. And what use do you think I'd be in the pit today with your nagging driving me daft?'

Rona watched him through half-closed eyes, and as she let her head drop on her arms and began sobbing, Tom made a weary gesture.

'Look, what time've we got to be there?'

'Nine o'clock bus,' she mumbled without raising her head.

'It'll be a rush. But get ready. I'll slip along and get Charlie James to take my shift. I know he'll do it.'

As she watched him go she sat up, sniffed, dried her eyes and began to gather up the breakfast things. They rattled on to the tin tray in a fanfare to the victory she did not even attempt to keep from her eyes. She moved about tidying up; perfunctorily, for her tidying, like her morning dressing, not being for public exhibition, was sketchy.

She left Tom's cap on the table, and with a glance at the clock went upstairs to change.

Sirens and buzzers hooted and life stirred noisily outside as she dressed, but she was unconscious of anything but herself, and she came downstairs humming a pop tune, satisfied in having her own way.

She was dressed in a cheaply smart costume, and her hair, coaxed into a suggestion of the newest style, managed to assert its natural untidiness as it straggled at the back from beneath an absurdly inadequate hat.

She frowned at the clock because Tom was not back yet, and her eyes foreshadowed a harrowing time for him should he let gossiping delay him much longer.

She put her compact on the oven top and stood tiptoe to see into the mirror over the mantelpiece, and was building up a too-perfect mouth in vivid red when the street door opened and Tom came into the kitchen. As through the mirror she watched him enter her mouth twisted sarcastically and she said: 'Taken plenty of time about it. I thought you weren't coming back.'

He stood by the door, looking steadily at her, and twisting a yellow rose in his fingers. Then he closed the door and went heavily to the nearest chair, and in a voice lifeless because it was so even, he said: 'I've come back.'

Rona watched his reflection as though there was something she did not understand. She went on with her making-up, then paused, lipstick held to her mouth, as she noticed the fixed way in which Tom was staring at her.

'You are coming to the wedding?' She said this uncertainly, and then clinging to the gaiety that was slipping from her, she added in forced defiance, 'You haven't got the whole pit closed for the day!'

'It is.'

Tom spoke simply, and Rona looked quickly at him through the mirror, suspecting humour. But fear crept into her eyes as she saw him leaning forward in his chair with his head buried in his hands.

The lipstick trailed off on its stroke, slipping upwards at the corner of the mouth, leaving Rona with a ghastly twisted grin.

'What happened?' she whispered.

'You haven't heard.' Tom was not asking; he spoke as though he knew Rona would have heard nothing but the schemings of her own mind this morning.

'Charlie did take my shift. He was pulling my leg about the wedding when he went off, and he gave me this rose for my buttonhole.'

Tom paused, staring at the floor, his mouth working at words that would not come.

'They'd just got out of the cage when it happened,' he said at last. He stood up suddenly and laughed. But the laughter was uneasy and had a hard sound to it.

Then his voice rose wildly, 'I'm ready,' he said, 'Charlie's crushed down there, but I am ready!'

She stood with the crimson grin livid in her white face. Unbelieving she began to back away, retreating from the realisation, but she could not escape from the horror in her husband's eyes.

He stood in front of her, silently, staring, his shoulders drooping as they would increasingly droop in the self-despising years ahead. Rona's hand went to her mouth, smearing the red stain. Although Tom did not speak the moment seemed fixed for ever.

Then the rose slipped from his fingers, and as he moved to pick it up his elbow caught against his cap which made a sharp tap with its peak as it fell to the floor and covered the yellow rose.

He reached out towards it, then letting his arm drop he turned away.

One Last Night

by

Lana Koster

She hadn't meant to kill him, it had just happened. It was true that she didn't like him much but she didn't hate him enough to make him die.

The chain reaction had started the night before when she had been sitting in a very non-descript bar in the West-end of London. He had just sat down beside her, he didn't look too bad, his blonde, just long enough hair was styled to a neat wave that nicely complimented his short, bristly beard that was very nearly 'five o'clock shadow'.

'Hi, my name's James, James Keel. Would you like a drink?'

She nodded. A few moments later he came back with a low alcohol beer for himself and a half-pint of cider for her. 'Thanks. My name's Elaine, Elaine Richardson.'

The chat had gone on for another hour or two (she couldn't quite tell, time had no meaning to her at the moment) over drinks. After the bar closed she had invited James back to her flat even though she didn't really know why, she just felt like having a fling with this rather good looking man.

When they got back to her flat she asked him to make himself at home while she slipped into something 'more comfortable'.

She went into the bedroom and started to undress. She put on a creamy/peach silk teddy, a long flowing dressing gown and a large spray of noxious perfume.

'After all,' she said to herself 'it'll only be wasted after tonight.' And with this puzzling statement Elaine swept out of the bedroom and into the living room where she hoped James was still waiting. He was still there and when she walked in he put down the photograph he was looking at and his hands strayed to his beard and started stroking his beard pensively.

'Wow ... you look ... wow ... I don't know what to say.'

'Don't say anything.'

Elaine sat on the sofa and carefully arranged the dressing gown to reveal an exquisitely shaped leg. James moved rather shyly across to the settee and sat down beside her. He put his large, heavy hand on her knee but she lifted it up and just held it in the air.

'Is anything wrong?' he asked.

'Oh. No. Everything's fine.' She said, appearing to be waking from a deep sleep. She let his hand fall back onto her knee, lay back and meant to let things happen. He moved in on her and meant to plant a firm kiss on her lips but before he could she darted away nervously.

'Are you alright?' He asked again.

'Mmmm. Fine.' She said, even though it didn't look like she believed herself.

'Are you sure you want me here?' He moved to go.

'No,' she said emphatically 'Please stay. Don't go.'

He sat down again and tried to relax. 'Shall we start again?' He asked.

She nodded and looked into his eyes. He moved closer again and this time she let him touch her lips. They kissed and he ran his hands through her hair. She seemed tense but toughed it out this time. But she just couldn't go on when he tried to touch her breasts. 'It's no good. I can't, I just can't.' She was about ready to cry.

'Is there something you want to talk about?' He asked, not really wanting to hear the answer.

'No, yes. Yes, I'm sorry, I don't even know why I invited you back here.'

James really didn't know what to do. Why him? Why should he be picked by some strange (but good looking, he had to admit that) woman to apparently perform only to be shot down as he's getting into his stride.

'Look, just sit down and tell me what's wrong.' He tried to sound comforting but didn't quite manage it.

'Well y'see, I was going to have a wonderful time. I was going to do everything I've never done before. In all of my 25 years I've never even come close to erm ... going all the way, to put it rather crudely ...' She stopped short.

'In all my life I don't think I have ever, ever, come this close to 'converting' a virgin.' James thought.

'I really do think you should go now,' Elaine said.

'No. I won't. I want to try and help you.'

Elaine looked at him suspiciously and, only naturally, wondered what his motives were.

'Just tell me about it,' he said.

They talked well into the early hours of the morning about a lot of things, all of which would be too lengthy and personal to tell anyone else, much too personal to tell a total stranger which of course they both were. Elaine didn't know how it happened but by the end of the night James had managed to pull down her inhibitions and get her into bed.

33

When she had woken up on the morning after 'the night before' she had been so confused. Words and visions that had been said and had happened the night before. She didn't know what to do anymore. She looked at the sleeping figure next to her in the bed and wept. What seemed like hours later but have been only minutes later, she got out of bed, wrapped the duvet around herself, and leaving James lying naked on the bed, went over the a chest of drawers in the kitchen and took something out of one.

When he woke up he could hardly remember anything, where he was, who he was with or what he had done last night. Then it all came back to him in a flood, the girl, the talk and then the sex. He looked around but couldn't see her. Then he heard something in the kitchen and got up to investigate. Before he went any further he put on his boxer shorts that were lying awkwardly on the floor. When he did finally get his boxer shorts on and managed to get into the kitchen he was met by a very disturbing sight. The girl he vaguely remembered as being called Elaine was standing at the window holding a very sharp, very long knife, pointing at her chest and staring into space.

'What the hell d'you think you're doing? Are you insane?' He screamed at her.

She hardly re-acted at all, just looked dreamily at him. He fairly ran towards her in an attempt to get rid of the knife. Instead of dropping the knife or even trying to stab him she started to plunge the knife into her own chest drawing a small bead of blood and a cry from James.

'Don't come any closer.' She threatened.

He stopped dead in his tracks. 'Just put the knife down. Calmly' he tried to reason with her, 'What's wrong? I thought we'd worked everything out.'

'You tricked me. You used me. I'm worthless.'

'No you're not. When we spoke last night you seemed 0so warm, so caring. I like you, alot.'

Her eyes seemed to soften slightly, he saw a tiny sliver of hope, if he could just reason with her. He held his hands up in a gesture of submission and stepped forward. She didn't move, just kept watching him.

'What makes you think I tricked you?'

She seemed confused by this question.

'I ... er ... I. You spoke kind words to me, then you just used me like a nobody.'

'No, really, I didn't. I wouldn't do anything like that.' He took another step closer.

'Stop that,' she whispered, 'stop it.'

Elaine reversed the knife so that the very, very sharp end was pointing towards James.

'It all happened so fast,' she would later tell her psychiatrist. 'He didn't see I'd turned the knife around, he almost ran towards me, probably wanting to disarm me. Anyway, I didn't know what he was doing and he was too fast, I couldn't drop the knife in time. I didn't want to kill him. He was so beautiful. The knife pierced his chest, blood everywhere. I didn't know what to do. He wouldn't die for ages. He just kept looking at me with those eyes, those beautiful eyes.'

The Hairdressers

by

Susan Morgan

'Excuse me, may I ask you a personal question?' To start with I did not lift my head, but as there was no answer I tried to to see why Giuido, usually so chatty, was not replying. It was no easy task, as he was busily twisting bendy rollers into my hair. I could just about see via the mirror in front that he was making no attempt to respond to the question. Then I realised that the question had been addressed to me!

I was used to being ignored in here as it always felt far more like a barbers shop than a hairdressers salon. The men all carrying on joking as the females were greatly outnumbered by them. I was the only female in this morning.

'May I ask,' came the voice again, 'your shirt, where did you get it?'

Squinting up at the mirror I now saw a very pleasant, sandy haired youth reflected there. Instead of replying I felt foolish as a sudden rush of blood to my face made me blush. I was so aware of the way I must look, head covered in multi coloured twists sticking out in all directions, and why oh why did the lighting shining down from the mirror, emphasise the bags under my eyes so much!

The face continued to look enquiringly at me. I noticed the strong jaw line, the cleft in the chin, the layer of carefully nurtured fine stubble (well I imagined that it was carefully nurtured). It gave the questioners face a youthful glow. 'Did you get it locally?'

At last I managed to reply, smiling weakly, 'Morgans, in that clothes department on the top floor.'

I let my eyes look downwards again, thankful not to be looking at my mirror image. The grey nylon wrap that Giuido always put on me, in that slightly sensuous way, was covering most of my clothes. It had slid off my one knee to reveal the opaque black tights that I was wearing with black denim shorts and red boots. I felt that the boots picked up the brightness of my big shirt which was loose over a black polo neck sweater.

'May I feel it?'

'Pardon?'

'Your shirt, may I feel it?' Again I could feel the flush on my face and wondered why I was reacting in this way.

The youth's hand reached out and slowly stroked the end of my shirt sleeve that was exposed.

'Amazing isn't it! Like a kind of rough satin.'

'More like a piece of old carpet!' Relieved at managing to answer without blushing, I continued, 'I suppose it is a bit loud for an old dear like me! Though I don't suppose that you can see much of it at the moment.' I thought of the vibrant red, green, yellow, blue and black in heavily vaguely Indian patterns, smaller on the front but that on the back formed two enormous concentric diamonds bordered with entwined leaves. I supposed that it was hard to miss, but I enjoyed wearing it, it was comfortable and cosy.

'I noticed it in the mirror when you walked in, and when I left after my haircut, I kept thinking about it, so I decided to come back and ask you where you got it from, I hope you don't mind?'

'No of course not,' I replied, rather uneasily.

'You two getting on alright, are you?' Giuido's heavily accented voice broke in,

'I've finished with your rollers, can I move you over now? Or am I disturbing something interesting!'

It was raining heavily when I left the studio theatre on Friday evening nearly two weeks later. 'Trust me,' I thought, 'just when I need my umbrella, I've left it behind.' So I pulled my black velvet collar up and wrapped my coat around me as tightly as I could and ran down the steps. I always parked my car at the rear of the theatre because of the limited space in the front. I raced along the side passage as fast as I could, but even so I felt pretty wet by the time I reached my car. The car park was almost deserted, just my grey Scirocco parked under the orange glare of the lamp and two cars in the shadows at the back. I had just put my key in the lock when I was aware of headlights being flashed, I looked up to see a car being driven fast through the car park entrance, the lights flashed again and with a squeal of tyres a sleek white BMW pulled up within inches of my car.

A youth jumped out, 'Hi, I don't suppose you recognise me?'

I looked and saw that same face that I had studied as a reflection in a mirror. 'You're the guy that was at the hairdressers, but what are you doing here?'

'I found out from Giuido that you were rehearsing for a play, then I found out the times, it wasn't difficult!'

'Yes, but why are you here?' That sense of unease I had felt before resurfaced.

'I came to find out what can be done.'

'I'm sorry, I don't understand.'

'What's to be done, your shirt, there aren't any left in the shop, they said they weren't likely to get any more, so I want to know what's to be done!' His voice was rising, I decided I did not like this situation.

'I'm sorry, but I think I'll go home now.' I started to get into my car but his hand grasped me tightly around the wrist, I gasped.

'You're wearing it tonight aren't you?' He pushed me roughly into my car and before I knew what was happening, he was in there too shoving me over to the passenger seat.

'This is ridiculous,' I started to say as I tried to unlock the passenger door but we were off, hurtling out of the car park, right across the traffic, barely slowing at the traffic lights we screeched left onto the ring road, through two more sets of lights, right again around the bend and then braked. He had stopped outside Giuido's.

As quickly as I could I got out of the car and started to run, 'Oh why isn't there anyone about!' He soon caught up with me, one hand clamped hard over my mouth, the other twisted my arm painfully. However hard I tried to kick and wriggle out of his grasp, nothing seemed to work.

He unlocked the heavy old wooden door, dragged me along the corridor up the creaking stairs turned left at the top and unlocked the next door into the shop itself, he pushed me in and slammed the door. He stood blocking my exit.

'I don't understand all this, now please let me go home.' I started to walk towards him, hoping that he could not see how much I was shaking, 'Come on don't be daft.' Before I got any further he grabbed me again. 'Did Giuido give you keys for this place? Why no alarms? How did you know that I was wearing my shirt tonight?'

'Shut up.' A towel tied tightly around my mouth prevented any more questions. 'Take your shirt off!' With fumbling fingers I unbuttoned my coat then my shirt, it seemed hopeless to try anything else.

'I'm good with locks, how do you think I got that white car you saw me in?' he talked as he busily trussed me up in two of Giuido's wraps.

'I came round here earlier and fixed the alarms, I've been watching you ever since I found out where you lived, I like to get what I want!' He sat me on the chair staring at that same mirror that I had first seen him in. Then came the pain, a searing pain that started in my back but that soon screamed throughout

38

my body. I saw the youth's back receding through the door, I heard the key turn in the lock, the footsteps down the stairs, the old wooden door bang shut. I was alone.

I looked at the black edged mirror surrounded with postcards, I saw my reflection. No rollers now, wet strands of hair hanging limply around my face, the bags under the eyes darker with streaked makeup, the pain and the towel twisting my mouth into a hideous grin. I wanted to reach out and touch my husband's hand, to kiss my daughter and son, but I was denied the comfort of human touch. I felt my spirit rise and leave my poor contorted body.

Giuido found my body the next day. The murder remained unsolved, apparently motiveless. No sign of sexual assault, no sign of robbery. Nobody thought of a bright overshirt.

But I feel robbed, robbed of my life, my family and of the chance to tell them that I am at peace.

Miss Stansfield

by

Janet Elizabeth Gasper

Miss Stansfield began teaching at the grammar school when I was in the fourth year. She was a thin, rather diminutive woman with whispy, light brown hair which seemed to drop in straight folds around her head and curl up slightly at the neckline. She had an unremarkable face, except for her eyes - clear blue eyes that shimmered with the sorrows and joys of the world and looked right into your soul.

I suppose she was about thirty at the time. My friends and I had little interest in the personal details of teachers unless it smelt of scandal - any hint of dark liaisons, illegitimate children, things of that nature and we were digging and delving for more, but we really cared little about the circumstances of those who faced us daily.

She came to school to teach Religious Studies - a subject which had effectively been off the curriculum for years. When the last qualified Divinity mistress had left, the subject had declined and the legally required weekly sessions were divided amongst the staff of other disciplines, who either did their own thing or told us to read or do homework.

Miss Stansfield was to teach every girl in the school - all classes for Religious Studies. She was to be in charge of class assemblies and charity fund raising and set up community work for the sixth form, and she was employed to do all that for less than half of the working week.

Looking back as I do now from my own lofty position as Head of English in a large school, I wonder why she took the job on such terms - there is no doubt she was exploited. She had no free lessons and must have put in hours of unpaid time. Now I am intrigued to know where she came from, details of her background, family and friends. Then it was irrelevant. We were not interested in teachers as people - we used them as the system dictated.

I suppose out attitude was partly born of the attitude towards us displayed by many of the older staff, who were not interested in us as individuals. There were too many of us in a group and there was not time. We were all caught up in the education sausage machine. We knew we were best quality offal, they, the aromatic spices at our disposal. All that counted was the product churned out at the end - a string of high grade paper qualifications that would give us admission to the next part of the process.

Miss Stansfield was teaching a Cinderella subject, a subject not offered for public examination. In our ignorance we believed that she could make no contribution whatever to our education. Her lessons, however interesting, were a waste of time and on that basis the poor woman was condemned before she had set foot over the threshold of our classroom.

She had a quiet manner - I suppose she was really too 'nice' to survive in teaching. She did not threaten or cajole us, and she certainly never 'grassed' on us. She begged and beseeched us, wrung her hands in despair and sighed deeply. We loved it - we had no real plan of campaign, but she just seemed to play into our hands.

Every now and then we would let her have a good lesson, when we would not shout out or purposely mess up the group discussion she had planned so carefully. In those sessions I was inspired by her - I realised that not only did she know a great deal about her subject (she could make any passage of the Christian Bible alive and relevant) but she could also see connections between bodies of knowledge. She was prepared to tackle the ultimate questions of life and she wanted to show us how literature, music, science, maths, art, history, all our examination subjects were trying to address these questions too. She wanted us to think about human values and feelings, free from the limits of a syllabus. How I wish now that I had allowed myself to sit at her feet.

But we were arrogant. We knew that examination results were all that mattered and so we plundered her pearls of wisdom and sabotaged her skills. We did it slowly and cleverly. We undermined her confidence - sometimes we did not even allow her to start a lesson. We talked, we hummed, we drummed our fingers on the desks, we dropped our tins of pencil crayons. Her carefully planned introductions were delivered falteringly, interspersed with pleas for silence. We refused to do the practical activities she had set out on workcards, which must have taken her hours to produce. We unashamedly handed in the most atrocious work and laughed at the 'encouraging' comments she gave it.

I do not know what went on in her other sessions. I think the younger children worked well for her and the sixth form liked her, but we did not care. Each lesson she came to us more timid, more outwardly nervous and she was clearly confused by our occasional cooperation.

One afternoon, she came a little late for our lesson. I caught a glimpse of her as she approached the classroom. I watched her forcing back her shoulders and

41

trying to gather herself for action. When she came in we shuffled out feet and nudged chairs against desks and shouted to one another.

I think I almost saw the thought of turning tail and running pass through her mind, but she just stood there and eventually we sat down. We set up more than our usual barrage of undercurrent noise, enough to put her off her stride, but not attract the attention of staff in other rooms.

I remember that her lesson was about how Christians understand the crucifixion. She wanted us to look at a newspaper report about a police woman shot by gunmen - she always started from the familiar and worked back to the theology. We threw the photo copies she had made around the room. We did not allow her a moment's silence. There was always one group of us talking or making noises. She gabbled something about notes in our books and then we knew we had her on the run.

We knew she was crying when she turned her back on us to write on the blackboard. We watched her slight figure shake as she raised the chalk, but we did not let up. We began to throw 'soggies' (chewed up bits of paper) at the blackboard, and then we aimed them directly at her, and hit her neck and as she turned round one hit her full in the face.

She stood with her arms stretched out and those eyes looking full at us and above her was the only word she had managed to write on the blackboard - Crucifixion.

'Yes,' she sobbed, 'this is what crucifixion is like - it's slow and painful and cruel. Do you think we have no feelings? If you prick us, do we not bleed?'

She sat down at the desk weeping quietly, but not for herself. She wept for us and the system that put us in this situation. We were like a pack of bitches in full cry, tearing the heart out of the lone exhausted fox.

We could have started up again, but we just sat there open mouthed. We had completely humiliated her, and yet, in her weakness, she seemed to exude a strength we had never imagined.

The bell went, she did not dismiss us. She gathered up her things and left the room quietly and with dignity.

After school I bought a large card. I don't know what made me choose it. On the front was the picture of a fox cub looking out from a broken down barn. I think it was the eyes, just like hers, open and loving but full of fear and hurt. I wrote the word 'sorry' in the centre of the blank page inside, and the whole class signed their names.

The next day we took our peace offering to the staffroom. It was taken from us unceremoniously by the senior member of staff who answered the door and who assured us it would be placed in Miss Stansfield's pigeon hole.

Next lesson, in her usual quiet manner, she thanked us for the card and said she would treasure it. We never played her up again, but she left soon afterwards at the end of term and we fell into the hands of the tyrannical Mrs Proctor, who knew nothing of religion or life, but never had any trouble in the classroom.

The Candlemas Fair

by

Jean Payter

'Where has that man got to?' Alice wondered, placing her hands on her ample hips peering through the kitchen window across the yard to the stable where her husband Frank had gone half an hour before.

It was Saturday, and every Saturday she and Frank and their three daughters dressed in their best clothes and rode in the open cart to town. Alice looked forward to these trips. Impatiently she lifted the latch on the back door and hurried across the yard, scattering hens as she did so.

Inside the dark dusty stable a sad sight met her eyes. Jasper, the old carthorse was a large still mound on the straw and Frank was squatting over him, furtively dabbing his eyes with a handkerchief.

'He's dead Alice,' he whispered sadly.

'I can see that,' she snapped, 'fancy him dying on a Saturday!'

Stunned by her insensitivity, Frank rose to his feet. 'He was a good horse Alice,' he said, 'no oil painting but a reliable, hard working horse.'

Alice wasn't listening. She turned and stumped away across the yard. Hhalf way she stopped and turned back. 'Frank!' she shouted, 'Isn't it the Candlemas Fair next week?'

Frank shrugged, 'What if it is, we haven't got a horse to get us there.'

Alice was not to be put off. 'That's no problem, pop up and see Fred Ray, he'll lend us a horse and get the knacker man to collect him,' she nodded towards the stable, 'while you're at it.'

Frank shook his head in wonder at her callousness and trudged slowly up the lane, his shoulders drooping.

Fred Ray was cleaning out the pig sty when he arrived.

'Fred,' he called, 'could you lend me Monty for the Candlemas Fair, old Jasper's been and died.'

Fred slowly shook his head. 'Monty's got a lump as big as an egg on his hock where the black gelding kicked him. Sorry mate.'

'Not to worry.' Frank turned to go.

'Ang on,' Fred called after him, 'you can take *him* if you like,' and gestured over his shoulder with his thumb to the black geldings' stable.

44

Frank dithered a little, glancing anxiously at the black hairy face that had now appeared over the lower door. Finally he said, 'Yes that'll be grand Fred, thank you. I'll be round first thing Monday morning.'

'In fact,' Fred went on, 'if you were looking for a horse to buy, I might consider selling him.'

Frank swallowed, 'Ah, well that's very good of you to offer him to me Fred, but my Missus is looking forward to a day at the fair, so we'll try there first, see you Monday,' and he was gone.

By good fortune, Monday dawned bright and clear with a little warmth in the early spring sunshine. As a special treat, Alice had let their three plump daughters, Emily, Rose and Jane have the day off school. Frank had fetched the black gelding and was adjusting the Jasper sized harness when Alice and the girls trooped across the yard.

'Heavens!' Alice exclaimed, 'couldn't you have found an uglier horse?'

A few minutes later they were rumbling along the narrow lane, the three girls squabbling in the back, Alice nagging incessantly to make the horse go faster. Frank, dressed in his best breeches and pigskin gaiters, brown lightly nailed boots and a flat pancake cap, hummed happily to himself and appeared not to notice.

They arrived just before lunch, clambering down from the cart and securing the black gelding, with his nose bag, to a convenient tree near the cattle pens. Huge Shire horses were being trotted up and down for prospective buyers. Young stock clattered on the road, being driven by young lads with whips from the horse boxes of the Station. Smart cobs for market, gardeners drays and Governess carts high stepped elegantly into the ring.

Frank was about to take a closer look at a sturdy roan, when, to his dismay, Sam West a local 'expert' appeared and clapped him on the shoulder.

'Frank, good to see you!' He bellowed. 'Shouldn't touch that roan if I were you, it suffered terrible with the founder last year.'

Frank went instead to examine the teeth of a large grey which promptly lifted it's head out of reach.

'That's because it's got the lampas,' Sam advised.

Frank sighed and moved towards a bony bay. Sam was there too. 'This one's supposed to have a dicky heart.'

Exasperated, Frank pointed to a heavy dun that a hopeful horse coper had led up for their inspection.

'I suppose this one's got a wooden leg,' he said irritably.

Sam roared with laughter and gave him a playful punch on the arm. 'You are a card Frank, course it 'asn't, 'tis blind in one eye though.'

'Heavens above,' thought Frank, 'it'll be hard to replace old Jasper.'

Sam was now plucking at his sleeve. 'Here's a nice horse Frank, just coming into the ring, being sold by a Vicar too, in favour of a car I ask you, no future in them things.'

Frank, a little bewildered by his companions non stop chatter, allowed himself to be propelled to the ringside.

'Chestnut cob mare,' the auctioneer sang out, 'fifteen hands, nine years old, quiet to ride and drive, sold sound. Who will start me at ten guineas?'

Someone started him at six and slowly the bidding crawled up to nine. Frank could see Alice on the other side of the ring obviously looking for him. She peered in his direction and he waved.

'I have ten guineas,' boomed the auctioneer, 'thank you sir. All done gentlemen?' and the hammer went down with a crash.

Frank turned ruefully to Sam, 'I didn't want a chestnut and I didn't want a mare,' was all he said.

Lady, as their new acquisition was called, was paid for and tied to the back of the cart for the journey home. However, the moment the cart began to move Lady dug her heels in and when she felt herself being dragged, she panicked and threshed about like a fish on a line.

'She'll never be as good as Jasper,' Frank remarked as he untied the mare.

Sam Weston had re-appeared. 'You'll have to ride her home,' he advised, 'I'll give you a leg up.'

Before Frank could object, Sam had grabbed his left leg and was boosting him upwards on to the mare's back.

Then to his horror, Frank noticed a gentleman on a grey hunter pull up alongside the black gelding while he called 'cheerio' to friends.

'Er, be careful,' Frank began, but was too late. The black gelding lunged surprisingly swiftly at the grey and sank his huge yellow teeth into it's neck. The other horse, deeply shocked by such unsocial behaviour, whirled around at speed, dumping it's rider with a thud on the hard ground.

'Time to be going,' Frank hastily urged the mare forward and Alice snatched up the driving reins.

The black gelding seemed to like Lady being just in front of him and he strode along purposefully, ears pricked, head bobbing up and down. Frank, looking back at him, wondered if he had fallen in love or whether he was just hoping to get a shot at her with those big yellow teeth of his.

The journey home was beginning to seem rather pleasant. They clip clopped past frowning thatched cottages and hedgerows starred with Primroses. The black gelding had decided Lady wasn't worth exerting himself over after all and was now some way behind, to Alice's annoyance.

Frank had discovered that Lady would only walk down the centre of the lane, rather than to the side, no doubt allowing for the customary cart. This didn't bother Frank unduly until, in a particularly narrow part, Major Bentley came steaming towards them in a pony and trap, waving his whip and shouting imperiously, 'Get out of the way man!'

Cursing silently, Frank slithered off Lady and dragged her into the side, respectfully touching his cap as the Major bowled by.

Frank then discovered that he could not remount. He led the mare to a gate and tried to fling himself at her back from the top bar but each time Lady adroitly side stepped.

'You cow!' Frank howled inaccurately. He desperately wanted to be on his way before the family caught up, but already he could hear the rumble of the cart and then he could see the black geldings' mulish face appearing round the bend.

'What's happened Dad?' The girls called happily.

'Just shut up and come and hold this mare!' He shouted back and then thought, 'she'll never be as good as old Jasper.'

They completed the journey home in comparative peace and the sun was beginning to sink in a reddening sky as the two horses clopped wearily into the yard.

Frank led Lady into the stable and filled the manger with hay. Then he unharnessed the black gelding and led him home. Fred was leaning over the pig sty wall scratching the sow behind her ears.

'You spend more time with that pig than with your Missus,' Frank remarked as he handed over the black gelding's halter rope.

Fred just grinned at him. 'You got yourself a horse then?' He asked.

'Yes,' Frank replied, 'a chestnut mare, just what I wanted.'

Fred began to lead the black gelding towards his stable. 'Well I hope she works out alright.'

'Oh, I'm sure she will,' Frank said confidently, 'in fact I reckon she'll be every bit as good as old Jasper.'

Death's a Buzz

by

Saul Saunders

Margaret stared, fascinated, at the fat black insect climbing leisurely up the kitchen window, her hands immersed in the washing up water momentarily stilled.

It seemed oblivious to her. Totally indifferent to her scrutiny. Only stopping occasionally to wriggle sensuously in the warmth from the sun.

She removed the remaining dishes from the water and stacked them carefully on the draining board, still keeping a watchful eye on the bluebottle. But it wasn't going anywhere. It was much too comfortable.

Opening a cupboard under the sink, she took out a can of fly spray and slowly removing the lid, directed the nozzle towards the contentedly buzzing insect, whilst pressing the nozzle firmly. Her smile was satisfied, as she witnessed the deadly spray's effectiveness. The insect buzzed angrily for a few seconds and then dropped onto the window sill.

That made five dead and three or four live ones still flying around in the living room to torment George, her husband.

She studied the writhing bluebottle interestedly. It wasn't giving up without a fight. Its legs were still moving and it buzzed intermittently.

She sneezed as the spray in the air irritated her sinuses, and leaned over the sink to open the window.

She heard their voices, loud and angry. George and Fred the elderly widower who lived next door. She almost laughed aloud when she heard Fred's angry protest.

'I keep telling you, they aren't mine,' he shouted. 'They're coming from somewhere else. Someone's compost heap probably.'

'Of course they're yours,' George retorted. 'You breed the filthy things don't you? For your fishing?'

The dispute had been going on for several months. George loathed flies and especially bluebottles. And in spite of all his efforts to repel them, they kept coming into the house.

'I breed maggots, yes,' Fred admitted. 'But they don't get out of my shed. I'll stake my life on that.'

Margaret giggled softly as she listened. It wasn't Fred's life that was at stake, was it?

'I'll see my solicitor,' George raged. 'I've had enough.'

But the solicitor could do nothing. And told George so quite bluntly.

'Can you positively identify them as your neighbour's bluebottles?' He had asked.

And George couldn't. Not positively.

So there was nothing he could do. Except rant and rave.

Margaret went to Bingo every Friday and contemplated it with particular excitement that morning, as she collected her groceries from the supermarket and called at the chemists for George's new prescription.

George didn't approve of her going to Bingo. And always grumbled about it.

'Mutton dressed as lamb,' he muttered that evening, as he watched her carefully applying lipstick.

Margaret ignored him and hummed to herself as she gazed in the mirror and quickly applied hair spray to her recently styled hair. A bubble of amusement rising in her throat almost made her choke. She was getting to be quite an expert with a spray. Accurate and decisive.

'And stop humming,' her husband snapped. 'You sound like one of those damned bluebottles.'

'Calm down George,' Margaret admonished him gently, as she delicately brushed her eyelids with silver eye shadow. 'You know what the Doctor said.'

'How can I forget when you keep on about it?' George snapped. 'I think everyone in the neighbourhood knows that I've got heart trouble.'

But of course they did. That was part of her plan.

'Did you get my prescription by the way?' He demanded.

Margaret frowned reproachfully at his reflection behind her in the mirror. 'Don't I always dear? It's in my other handbag, the brown one, in the wardrobe. I'll leave the bottle on the dressing table for you.'

George nodded. 'I'm going downstairs to watch television.'

She had only once forgotten to give the tablets to him. When they had been on holiday. She had put the new bottle in her handbag, after collecting it from the chemists. And then left her handbag in the hotel room when they went down to the beach.

And George had lost his temper with some yobbos, as he called them, playing football on the beach.

It had been touch and go.

49

But he had recovered.

And that was when she started to form her plan.

She popped her head around the living room door as she shrugged into her best coat.

'I've left you some sandwiches dear,' she said brightly. 'In a lunch box near the kettle.'

George didn't take his eyes off the television. 'Right,' he muttered.

'See you later then.'

'I'll be in bed.'

She rather doubted it.

Letting herself out of the house, she buttoned up her coat against the cool night breeze and walked briskly down the garden path towards the gate. She looked forward to her Bingo. And especially she looked forward to having a drink with her friend afterwards.

The television was still on when she opened the front door several hours later.

That was a good sign.

Hurriedly she searched the ground floor rooms. The lunch box was lying in the middle of the floor in the kitchen. But George was nowhere to be seen.

She moved quickly to the stairs. Supposing - supposing he had found the tablets. But he hadn't. He was lying on the floor in the bedroom. Quite dead. Margaret shuddered. Another minute or two and he might have found them.

Her brown handbag was on the shelf at the top of the wardrobe. Behind a shoe box. You could hardly say it was hidden. She quickly took out the bottle of tablets and put it on the dressing table. George's body was lying just a few feet away.

'I told him,' she would agonize. 'I begged him to keep his tablets with him all the time.'

She hurried back downstairs and into the kitchen.

She picked up the lunch box. She would have loved to have seen George's face when he'd opened it. She found the bluebottles quite easily. They were scattered about the room. All dead. Those 'Zap' space insect destroyers were impressively potent.

She scooped the dead bluebottles back into the lunch box and did a quick count. She had put thirty or so in. Now all she had to do was put them back in the greenhouse for the time being.

'If he had kept his tablets on him, he would probably still be alive,' George's Doctor sighed.

'I told him,' Margaret burst out, seemingly overwrought. 'I said, put them in your pocket. I blame myself,' she moaned. 'I should have been here.'

'Not at all,' the Doctor murmured soothingly. 'You couldn't watch him all the time. And besides, he was a grown man, responsible for his own actions.'

Margaret dabbed at her eyes with her handkerchief. 'I shall never forgive myself, never... ' her voice trailed off, 'My poor George.'

The Doctor patted her shoulder. 'Try not to upset yourself my dear.'

Margaret managed a tremulous smile.

'I've made out the death certificate,' the Doctor continued briskly, obviously of the opinion that enough sympathy had been dispensed. 'Natural causes of course.'

Margaret nodded, with bowed head.

She gazed happily at her reflection in the dressing table mirror the next morning.

The undertaker had been and taken George away.

And tomorrow morning very early, she would take the trays of maggots from the greenhouse and drive out into the country and get rid of them.

The greenhouse had been a marvellous hiding place, because George never went in there. He'd always hated gardening and his first heart attack had been the perfect excuse to give it up completely.

Life would be very different from now on. She would have the insurance money. Fifty thousand pounds and all hers. And she would be free to go where she liked, when she liked. And she could see her friend more often. He would be pleased about that.

And poor old Fred would be able to breed his maggots in peace.

She didn't need to go far. Any convenient ditch would do.

There were few cars on the road. It was still early, the sun rising in the East shining directly into her eyes.

Impatiently, she pulled down the sun visor.

And screamed.

The spider was huge. And it landed on her lap. She had always been terrified of them. Her hands left the wheel and flapped frantically at the monster, her body convulsing rigidly in shock.

51

The car veered off the road, glanced off a tree and rolled over several times dislodging its contents.

It rated a small paragraph on the front page of the local paper - headed 'Weird Death Crash - Woman Killed in Bluebottle Infested Car.'

Fred read it. And scratched his head and frowned as he tried to make sense of it. First George Fletcher and two days later, his wife.

Still, it was nothing to do with him. The bluebottles in Mrs Fletcher's car weren't his bluebottles. He'd stake his life on it.

Moments in a Middle-Aged Life

by

Romayne Mary Peters

Looking out of windows had become a bad habit and long discourses with herself another compulsion. Angelina felt that she had failed in every possible way and time was not merely running out, but laughing right back in her face. She had become self obsessed, making herself believe that she was the woman she had always imagined. It had nothing to do with beauty. She simply felt the spell of her own attraction; it may have been the expression in her eyes or dark tone of her voice or even the distinct singularity of her mind. But it had all added up to nothing and no one. Sometimes the fury of her frustration was a balm compared to her pain at rejection; the inevitable dust and ashes of disappointment.

'Sometimes you make me feel as though I had imagined it all,' she had said once, no matter now to whom and he had replied how impossible it was for him to be as he would prefer. He was not free to display his affection, but it did not mean he didn't love her. So what it actually meant, she would never know. The absurdity of their involvement had not been lost on Angelina. In her rational moments she recognised that he had seemed almost stupid in the most ordinary way, but like most women, she had been able to make of him what she believed was required of him by her functioning mind and body, so while he remained the man that he always was, she had created a lover and a lover is what she saw.

'Surely you can find time to write me some lines on office paper, just once in a while. You always say you love hearing from me and I love writing. I have to write when I'm bursting to talk. It's like throwing my body into the words, so that you can feel me; feel the intensity of my need to speak to you.' But she'd more or less said most of this before. He'd occasionally speak to her on the phone. The voice was sometimes warm, but nothing of real significance could be said. A few staccato sentences, but no information except it could sound non-committal, in the event of other ears also listening.

She was invariably angry at her lack of pride. Always had been. She remembered deciding each time she fancied that she'd found a man to interest her that she must learn to realise that the things that mattered to a woman, meant nothing to a man. For while a man will think about a woman when he needs a woman, a woman thinks about a man the whole damned time.

'Angelina,' her mother called.

Her mother was very old and lived with her now, demanding attention at the slightest pretext and where there is no love, duty has to double for it. So that Angelina did all that was necessary without ever touching her mother with a gentle gesture that would have pleased the old woman. 'You never do something spontaneously for me,' her mother had reproached her once. Not thinking, that if there was a constant and endless stream of requests, very little was left about which to be spontaneous .

How had it all happened? Childhood had seemed so sure. She had been happy. She had been protected. Nobody had spoken about the real world. The obviousness of being happy ever after was the most foregone of all conclusions.

The taking of those vows for better or worse, in boredom and in stealth until marriage tears apart had never-the-less inducements that bound her still. She was now more faithful to herself though and that was easier for her than the man enrolled to do the cherishing. To have an honourable husband had the drawback of making life too serious. He thought so much about their welfare in the years to come, that the here and now had lost all excitement. Angelina knew that she had a lot for which to be thankful, but how can one be grateful for something that one doesn't want.

It was when she was just past thirty, that the struggle began. She felt the need to stir the waters of that pool that's called desire. To throw the stone out far and see the ever widening ripples reach out until they touched her. Upbringing became meaningless, her mother's values were for some other daughter. Nothing was the same again. She had seen the eyes of a man with the look of intent. The search should have been over, but it had only just begun. An imagination captured is dangerous indeed, for astride ones brain sits the phantom that in time, one finds, cannot be located anywhere else.

Looking out of windows. That was all that was left; that and errands for her mother; contrived interest in her future welfare and the ludicrous and on going temptation that a smile may be returned if the genie, one day, shone the lamp so bright that she could be reflected in it as she really was and the creature astride her brain came out in instant recognition and she would be alone no more. Loneliness is as much a condition of being in a room full of the wrong people as being isolated in a cell.

So the windows are all there. The leaves all turning; some scarlet, some gold. Here and there gnarled branches. Some of the trees quite old.

Alone

by

Mary Norton

As she walked she felt the ground cushioned by a mass of leaves and pine needles, her step was silent because of this. The view ahead was of a multi-coloured carpet strewn across the pathway. Monty was ahead exploring nooks and crannies which had been covered until his nose had sought them, returning only to check if she was walking towards him. His amber coat blended as a camouflage against his surroundings.

Why did she have to leave all this? The place she loved, her dog which meant so much to her. It had all been thought out logically and deep down she knew it was the right thing to do - get away - away from memories and to start again.

She called Monty and started to retrace her steps back to the cottage at the edge of the woods. The cottage which had been lovingly restored, each room was planned so carefully, it had almost been rebuilt inside. 'For what, she felt now, for what?'

The gate was reached and Monty bounded through the garden which was perfect now, neatly laid lawns with beds full of autumn colour. What a comparison to when they had first viewed it; weeds, brambles and grass entwined to block their way; a path had to be hacked through it to reach the door. Now inside it was warm and snug, Monty made himself comfortable on the rug by the log fire. She sat looking at the furniture around her, saying a mental farewell to her so familiar surroundings, only a few more personal items had to be packed as a lot of it was going into store until she came back - If I do - she thought.

The contract had originally been for a year but she had been able to persuade them to half it just in case she didn't like it. She had been warned that journalism in America was so different to this country she thought back to when she had changed from writing for the local paper to one of the nationals. She was petrified in case she couldn't handle it and yet it came so easily - too easily in fact - that's why she realised that there was undiscovered talent lying dormant inside her. But it had taken a lot to decide to do something about it; for she had been so happy, idyllic really.

Robin could be blamed for it all, for making her happy, content and dependent. Too dependent though she had left her career to flounder to promote his. He had overwhelming ambition, such a flare for creativity that he overshadowed everyone or at least made them feel he did.

How long had it been now since they met? 'Five years', she thought. It was at a promotion campaign which he had organised, it was her job to interview this up and coming executive. It was almost love at first sight such a mutually overwhelming experience for them, she had never left his side since that evening. They planned together, worked together and their future was almost pre-arranged. She had decided to sell her flat and move into his, so they could buy the cottage as well as having a flat in London, to 'stay over'. When the cottage was ready they moved, just leaving the bare essentials in the flat. Her house warming present was Monty, a fluffy amber bundle of fur.

Everything was wonderful, for a long time she had given up commuting and posted stories to the paper, as now she had her own column and much preferred the countryside to the hustle of the big city. But Robin's staying over in London had become more frequent over the last six months. ·

It was easy to make excuses to herself 'he was busy at work, a lot of people to see.' In fact she had almost convinced herself it was okay but there was a nagging doubt which kept prompting her to go and check.

She shuddered as she thought of it. She had planned to go to the flat and cook a special candle lit meal for them. She did the shopping first of all and was going to phone Robin to tell him, then decided a surprise would be more romantic. She made her way to the flat but it was she who had the surprise, no, a shock - Robin was already there in bed and he wasn't alone.

Tears came to her eyes as she remembered the humiliation that she'd felt. That was two months ago and it still hurt. She had thrown the shopping down and had just run away and she was running still.

Monty stirred and brought her back to reality. Why should she keep remembering? She noticed Monty had risen from his chosen place by the fire and had gone to the door, ears pricked as if expecting someone. She knew the house keeper wasn't due until the morning and the tenant to whom the cottage was leased wasn't arriving until Saturday. It made her realise how alone she was out here away from civilisation.

She jumped when the knock came on the door. Monty didn't bark, instead he was whimpering and scratching madly at the door. That made her feel slightly at ease because he would have barked incessantly had it been a stranger.

Cautiously she unlatched the bolt and opened the door slightly, just enough to see who was standing there. To her horror it was Robin; with a bunch of red roses not quite knowing what to do.

He had been too frightened of rejection to contact her after the incident, but when he had heard she had resigned from the paper and was off to America he knew he couldn't let her go without asking her one question - one which should have been asked a long time ago and to which he prayed the answer would be 'Yes.'

The Agony of Infidelity

by

Elizabeth Caton

Why? Why did I do it? To sleep with my husband's best friend. Not only his best friend, mine also.

We used to go everywhere together, he was as necessary to our lives as we were to each other.

I remember when we first met him, Paul, my husband grew quite jealous because Cameron and I became such good friends, so quickly. But he needn't have worried, not then. I knew Cameron was attracted to me, it lent a certain spice to our relationship but I wasn't physically attracted to him and I was desperately in love with my husband.

It didn't take long for Paul to become accustomed to the situation. He trusted me. How hollow those words sound now!

Paul and Cameron were very alike in some ways. They were both 'lads'. But while most lads when they get married carry on their lifestyle but leave their wives at home, Paul didn't. I was just as much one of them, as if I were in actuality a 'lad'! It was a good life while it lasted. When we went out, we all went out drinking and playing cards all night. I don't know whether you'd call me a feminist or not, but I've always hated double standards. I see no reason why I should be treated differently because I'm a woman. Inevitably, I suppose pressures came to bear in the form of Paul's friends. Not all of them. Who complained to Paul that they wanted to go out on 'all boys' night and however much I tried to be one of them, I simply wasn't. So I got left at home. Although the attitude might annoy me, it didn't bother me being left on my own. I'm a far more solitary person than Paul and I can always find something to occupy me. I have far too many other interests to enjoy going to the pub every night.

But one day, a friend came to visit me, Sue, who let slip that all the other girls pitied me because Paul was out drinking all the time and leaving me on my own. Before this, I had been content with my life but knowing that other people pitied me, really made me angry, not with them but with Paul for putting me in this situation.

So that's when the trouble between Paul and I started. For two years we had never quarrelled, in some ways to me, we had a perfect relationship. But now

Cautiously she unlatched the bolt and opened the door slightly, just enough to see who was standing there. To her horror it was Robin; with a bunch of red roses not quite knowing what to do.

He had been too frightened of rejection to contact her after the incident, but when he had heard she had resigned from the paper and was off to America he knew he couldn't let her go without asking her one question - one which should have been asked a long time ago and to which he prayed the answer would be 'Yes.'

p. 60 missing.

'The rotten little bitch! How dare she?' All of a sudden I was screaming angry.

'Caz, you can't blame just her, everyone in the pub could see something was going to happen weeks ago.'

'He told me he loved me, he left on Saturday morning, just after we'd made love and he told me he loved me!' I think I must have been hysterical, I just couldn't think coherently at all.

Sue was wonderful, she went out and bought a bottle of brandy. I just carried on drinking and crying until I passed out. The next two weeks passed like one eternal nightmare and all the time I just couldn't stop crying. In the end, I rang my father and asked him to pick me and my dog up, I just couldn't stand it any more.

My parents were brilliantly supportive. After several more weeks had passed, I had started to recover my spirit and feel angry but I still loved him. He'd started to ring me again, giving the flimsiest of excuses, which quite amused me. So for several months I kept him dangling, quite deliciously, I really did enjoy it. So much for any nobleness of spirit!

And so, after several months we started living together again. After several more months, it started happening again. He'd disappear for days drinking. But this time I did mind. I started to hate him. I think this is when my infatuation with Cameron started. I don't know whether infatuation is the right word, but whatever it was, it was strong enough for me to seek Cameron out and eventually tell him how I felt. Please don't think this was entered into lightly, it wasn't. Cameron and I discussed it from every angle. Of course, Cameron loved me, but he didn't know whether he was in love or whether it was strong enough for him to face the consequences of Paul's feelings when I left him.

We eventually decided to put it on hold. If we left each other alone for several months after I left Paul, then it would be quite respectable and not least of all Paul would not be able to accuse Cameron of stealing me off him.

Unfortunately nothing ever goes to plan, at least not in my life! Paul went on another bender and I succumbed to temptation. I went to Cameron's house at six in the evening and left at nine o'clock the next morning. I'm not ashamed of what happened. Whatever happens now, I will still have the memories of that one night. That sounds so mawkish! We had a wonderful time, playing cards for hours to determine who'd make the next pot of tea, doing crosswords together, laughing, and making love, of course. No, I'm definitely not ashamed of what happened. It was very special. We hadn't spoiled our friendship at all, we'd added a new depth to it in some strange way.

Again, it was unfortunate that Paul had curtailed his activities that night and had come home to find me absent. It's the lies that make it sordid.

Several days later, I saw Cameron and he told me haltingly that although he'd thought of nothing else and he did love me, he wasn't sure whether he was in love and he wasn't sure that he wanted to give up his bachelor life for me. So - that's the end.

I don't blame him. I forced the issue to a point of no return.

So now I ask myself - What do I do now?

It keeps flickering through my mind, if I am or was truly in love with Cameron or whether it was my subconscious nudging me to get my own back on Paul. I don't know, only time will tell, I suppose.

If anyone asked me if it was worth it, then the answer is No! Without a doubt, not because of the affects on anyone else concerned, but the emotional trauma you would be storing up for yourself.

Nor the Years Condemn

by

Anthony Collier

'Age shall not weary them, nor the years condemn.' Alice Downes had heard these words on November the eleventh for the past forty years, and the more she heard them the more she condemned him for enlisting, he hadn't needed to, he was in a reserved occupation.

Albert, Alice's husband had worked on a farm, and Alice had come to work there as a land-girl. It was love at first sight, Alice loved Albert with every fibre of her body. He had black curly hair, and a sun tanned complexion. It was his hair that attracted her, mainly because all the male members of her family had been bald. She remembered her grandfather's shiny head and her father had gone bald when she was little. So Albert's black curls really captured her. After a short courtship they were married and a year later Bertie was born, who made their happiness complete, so why did Albert have to enlist. She remembered how he came in and sat by her and took her hand, she felt her wedding ring slowly revolve around her finger. He always did this to her ring, whenever he felt sheepish, or, if he was about to tell her something that she wouldn't want to hear.

'What have you done.' She asked accusingly.

'I've been thinking.' He said. 'How long would this war last, if everyone shirked their responsibilities, I feel that I should be out there helping us to win.'

'You are helping to win, someone has to keep the home fires burning. Who would take care of me and Bertie?'

'All those men fighting have wives and children. I'm sorry, I feel that I must go.'

Alice knew that his mind was made up, so didn't pursue the argument.

'Just promise, that you won't get killed.' She pleaded.

'I promise, and no one will do more to keep that promise than me.'

When Alice received the telegram saying that Albert had been killed in action, she was consumed with grief, and remained in a state of shock for more than a year, even when her sister Emmie, suggested that Bertie stayed with some friends of hers she was in no condition to argue.

Emmie had always been jealous of Alice, and had got tired of looking after her baby, when her friends, Mary and Steve Jones came to collect Bertie, Alice was in bed. Alice would have asked after Bertie, but Emmie kept telling her not to worry. The day came when she felt that she could take care of Bertie, she asked Emmie where he was.

'It would be unfair to take him from his mother after all this time.' Emmie told her.

'But I'm his mother, and I want him back.'

'You try telling him that you are his mother. You would do irreparable damage to his mind to take him off Mary, and she does want to adopt him. If you love him you will agree. Emmie was a bully, and Alice was no match for her. She had a nervous break-down, and barely remembers the adoption being finalised.

Alice spent the next thirty years wondering what had happened to her son, and every time she mentioned it to Emmie, it was always met with, 'You'll only make yourself ill again, I should put him out of your mind.'

But Alice couldn't put him out of her mind, he occupied her every thought. She wondered if he was married, and if he had inherited his father's nervous habit of turning his wife's wedding ring.

When Emmie died, Alice decided she would devote her life to looking for him. She travelled miles but always kept drawing blanks. She had discovered that Mary and Steve Jones had three children of their own and had been divorced. She hadn't even known if they had given Bertie their name.

She felt hatred for her sister, and she hated herself for being weak, if only she had been stronger and stood up to her. She had found out that the Jones's children, including Bertie, had been evacuated to Wales, she went there and made enquiries. She spoke to a lady whose mother had looked after some children called Jones, she had said that the one boy had black curly hair, she believed that his name had been Victor. She pursued this line and discovered that he had been adopted by someone called Brownlow, but she couldn't find out if he was definitely her son, and if he was, she couldn't find out where the Brownlows where now. She wondered why, if the Jones's had got divorced, they hadn't offered to give Bertie back to her, or perhaps they had, and Emmie had said that she was in no fit state to look after him. She blamed herself for being devastated by her husband's death, a lot of herself had died with him.

Someone suggested to Alice that she should try the Salvation Army to see if they could help. She was introduced to a Major Ainslie, who promised he would do his best to find her son. A few days later an Officer from the Salvation Army called to see her, his name was Ralph Peterson.

'We have found a nephew of the Brownlows, we can't be certain that Victor was your son, but at least, if he isn't, then we can eliminate him from our enquiries and start again.'

Alice liked Ralph, he seemed such a caring man.

'I have arranged to meet the nephew tonight, I wondered if you would like to come, you will be able to shed more light on the matter than I could on my own.'

Alice said that she would be happy to go.

Alice felt exited, but also nervous, as she waited for Ralph to pick her up, supposing that her son didn't want her to come into his life, but she put such thoughts out of her head.

They arrived at the house and the nephew asked them in.

'I'm afraid that I can't be of too much help because I didn't have a lot to do with my aunt and uncle, but I seem to remember they had adopted a young boy who they called Victor, all I remember about him is that he had black curly hair, and was shy.'

Alice felt guilty about the boy being shy, it was due to the insecurity that she had forced upon him.

'Where is he now?' She asked.

'My aunt and uncle both died when he was a teenager, so where he went then I don't know, but I'm sorry to have to tell you this, someone said that he was in Kenton.'

'Kenton, that's a prison isn't it?' Alice asked.

'Yes, but we can't be certain that it is your son, we could be on the wrong track altogether.' Ralph said trying to reassure her.

'If he is in prison then it is my fault. I was the one who deserted him.' Alice had convinced herself that it was her son. 'Can we go and see him?' She asked Ralph.

Without knowing what he was in prison for, Ralph thought it better if he went alone. He took Alice home and promised that he would go to the prison the next day to make an appointment.

'I will stand by him no matter what he has done, there will always be a place for him here.' She told Ralph.

He went the next morning to see the governor of Kenton prison and was horrified to learn that Victor Brownlow was in prison for sexually assaulting children. He went to the citadel to see Major Ainslie.

'I just can't believe that dear old lady could have produced that monster.'

'Could you try to prove that it isn't her son, then you wouldn't have to tell her.'

'I would do anything to prove that, but I promised her that I would go and tell her today.'

He felt sick with worry as he walked up her path.

'What has he done, has he robbed someone?' She asked.

Ralph sincerely wished that he could have answered yes to that question.

'No he hasn't robbed anyone.'

'Well whatever he has done, I'm to blame.' She said.

Ralph's heart was heavy. 'You musn't blame yourself,' he told her.

How could this repulsive character be related to the dear old lady that he had become so fond of. The fact that he had been adopted couldn't be the reason for committing this abhorrent crime. Ralph had himself been adopted for a short while before going into an orphanage. He didn't even know what his real name was and had taken the name of the house-parent. He had been told that his real mother had committed suicide after being left a widow. He stroked his bald head and gently took her hand to break the distasteful news.

Alice knew then, that her searching was over as she felt her wedding ring slowly revolve round her finger.

Crush

by

Melanie Shaw

'And last, but by no means least, we have the lovely Isabel who is going to entertain us with a measure of mimicry, a treat of take offs and an imagery of imitations!' The blond Adonis waved his tanned arm in my direction as the lights miraculously dimmed to leave a circle of bright dazzling whiteness. In reality it was a single spotlight full of stagnant smoke. The noise in the 'Sunshine Social Club' blurred into a hum of expectancy and relief as the final act took to the stage. All eyes, even those who couldn't focus on anything other than the glass in their hand, turned to watch....me.

Craig pushed me forward with the palm of his hand firmly on my bottom. The touch that I had been seeking coming when I couldn't enjoy or respond to it.

The murmur gained depth, rumbled and then vanished completely leaving a silent pit like a black hole in space which consumes whole galaxies never to be seen again. It had an alluring ring to it, 'Never to be seen again.'

My mouth opened and I worded a greeting. A voice that was not my own croaked to a halt. I coughed like a non-smoker entering a Working Mans Club. At the side of the stage the compere was exercising his charms on the previous turn. I peered into the darkness trying to see invisible faces. I ran before the eyes had a chance to bury me.

I ran past the 6ft 4ins of prime manhood for whom this charade had been entered, past the mass of small children who looked like stranded fish with mouths all agog, through the blurred eyes wavering at the bar and out into the cool June evening. I was crying as I ran as far from the gaudy lights of the bar and stage as fast as I could. My eyes were stinging as the tears and make-up ran down my face, still I ran towards the beach until the softness of the sand and the highness of my heels brought me to a standstill 10 yards from the sea where I collapsed, all energy spent.

Needless to say I cried. Not at the embarrassment of my debacle in front of the biggest audience in the clubhouse all week (they probably wouldn't recognise me when sober) nor because it had all been witnessed by the object of my infatuations for the last seven days. I cried because I knew I was a fool who had bitten off more than I could get in my mouth let alone chew. It had been so easy to persuade me to enter that contest.

I still had another full seven days before my brother Jim would come to my rescue. The holiday had all been his idea. He was trying to protect me by playing at big brother. He saw it as the way for me to escape the torture of having a crush on a friend of his who broke hearts as often as he broke wind. He was no great catch but had the knack of making a girl feel wanted and needed. I later found that his lack of grace was the main reason for the large number of ex-girlfriends. The hiding or timing of such an event was as foreign to him as a Peruvian nose flute.

I had forgotten all about him three seconds after getting off the coach when my new idol had carried my small case into reception. He made me think that I was his deliverance from another boring week of playing to people's egos. Little knowing he was giving me his well rehearsed arrival performance. It wasn't out of the frying into the fire but more from one hot plate to yet another.

My thoughts returned to the show. I didn't know then why my hero had goosed every contestant whether male or female as they emerged from the shadows to the side of the stage. He was, as Jim put it later, open to any offer from any direction. It certainly hadn't relaxed me and it had reduced the first contestant to a quaking blancmange. Quite a feat for when you realise that he was a six foot sporty type. He had never looked at anyone except the compere during his entire nervous wavering rendition of Roy Orbison's 'Only the lonely.' He was absolutely terrified His favourite dream turning into his worst nightmare with a single pinch, the meaning of which he had understood better than I. He too had disappeared from sight as soon as Craig had released him from his shoulder clinch when the song faded to an embarrassing close. Craig did not want to let the act escape from his private public hell thus making himself appear a true professional by comparison.

I recalled his face and it made me smile. He was actually quite handsome but the torments being inflicted had made him seem so innocent and helpless. I chuckled to myself and then openly as the silliness of the whole thing came into view like the punchline of the self inflicted practical joke that it was.

I lay back on the cold damp sand with my arms flung out from my side chortling away not able or wanting to stop the flow of memories as I recalled a week of trailing the Superman from pillar to post. It was an emotional cleansing process.

I had entered the swimming gala, the treasure hunt and anything where I knew that Craig might be involved. The only time I'd felt a hint of success was when he had asked me if I had any talent at all. I had failed miserably in everything mainly due to his unnerving presence. I replied, with too much excitement to realise the consequences of my impetuosity, that I was known to my friends as a bit of a Mike Yarwood. I failed to add that I could only 'do' friends and relatives, a group which includes no-one famous and who all have my accent.

I lay on the beach unashamedly cackling at the faces I had pulled in the bathroom mirror in the last thirty six hours. Trying with increasing desperation to get my voice or my face to resemble Mrs Thatcher on the basis that everyone can 'do' Mrs T. I found that my Mrs T bore a closer resemblance to Mr T from the 'A Team' on television.

I sat up still grinning and wiping my eyes to witness the first act walking out of the sea towards me fully dressed, drenched and dripping, removing the bits of seaweed stuck to his legs.

'Go on. Laugh. Everybody else did so why not you too!' His voice wobbled with despondency mingled with fury.

'I'm not laughing at you, I'm laughing at me and my stupidity,' I replied looking him up and down. 'What happened to you?'

'You saw what happened.' He snapped quite unnecessarily I thought.

'But you weren't wet then!' I failed to suppress a giggle.

'Well I wasn't wearing high heels like you. I just kept running and the sea, not the sand, stopped me.'
He glared at me in a way that made me feel uncomfortable. Like I was a child again. It then became apparent to me from his condition that he had not seen my performance.

'Don't worry,' I said, 'by the time they have finished laughing at me they won't even remember that you were on and going by the other acts you might collect first prize when you get back.'

The look on his face was the same as that when he had been goosed. Horror and dismay merging to produce eyes that searched for understanding and help.

I told him what had happened from beginning to end, my crush, my infatuation, my downfall. Why I told him it all I don't know. He just let me talk as if he was an old friend helping me through a bad patch. Nodding at the right moments and staying silent when appropriate.

'So you entered the contest to try and impress him?' He asked with a certain glee when I had finished. Until then I thought he was being sympathetic so my reply was not polite.

Now it was his turn to roar with laughter as though no-one could hear. I jumped to my feet and stormed back up the beach. Full of anger and disbelief that yet again I had started to get a crush on a complete stranger in less than ten minutes. Would I never learn.

'Roy Orbison' caught me by the steps from the beach.

'It's so funny. If you weren't laughing at me but at yourself why aren't you laughing now.'

He smiled at me. 'I only entered the competition because I wanted to impress you. I've been following you around all week and you haven't taken your eyes off that creep once. It's so funny....'

He stopped short, his brain registering what his mouth had said. He opened his mouth but the brain got there first this time and he closed it. I looked at him, mimicking his movements. My jaw moving slightly up and down as if I could somehow coax the right words to the surface. It was like looking in a mirror. Uncertainty on our faces, warmth in our eyes and then wide wide smiles.

Waiting

by

Suzanne Johnson

It was suffocatingly hot in the room. Stephanie stood near the window to catch the wisp of air which crept lazily through the sliding panels of the double glazing. Her husband, Brian, fidgeted on the edge of the chair nearest to the door, nervously flicking through the pages of a newspaper.

Stephanie could see that it was several days old. She would have teased him about it on any other day... but today was different. It was a day they had been waiting for. They had prayed together for many months for this slim chance that could relieve their ever-increasing misery.

Brian cleared his throat. Stephanie looked up, hoping that he would say something, anything to break the awful silence. As if in answer to her thoughts, a church clock from somewhere nearby struck four.

They had been waiting helplessly now, for three long hours. The stifling silence continued and Stephanie, unable to watch Brian's restlessness any longer, turned to look out of the window. Was it really only this morning when the summons had come and the final decision had to be made... a cruel choice which could mean life or... Stephanie shuddered.

She noticed a fly which had landed on the window sill outside. It seemed to be deciding which way to go. At last it started to make its way along the channel between the panes of glass. Stephanie watched it, fascinated as it reached the end and disappeared into the dark corner of the window frame. She waited for what seemed an age for it to reappear.

Suddenly there was a frantic 'buzz' and she saw that the unsuspecting fly had walked right into the trap of a waiting spider who had responded instantly to the touch on its web. It was already busily spinning a cocoon of fine thread around the unfortunate insect. Stephanie had no love for flies but she felt surprisingly shocked as she witnessed the cruel end of the tiny life. For a few seconds she had almost forgotten her own desperate situation.

Brian was studying the only picture in the room. He gazed at the Lowry reproduction with unseeing eyes. It mattered nothing to him where all the figures were bustling to and from. He cleared his throat again and attempted to say something, but his voice sounded high-pitched and strange.

71

He tried once more. 'How... how long do you think they'll be?'
Stephanie studied her watch for the hundredth time.

'I wish to God I knew... I didn't think it would be as awful as this.'
They both turned their heads towards the door at the sound of footsteps approaching in the corridor outside. Stephanie felt herself go cold, even though her hands were still clammy from the warm air in the room.

She wasn't sure whether she felt relieved or even more agitated than before as the footsteps passed the door and continued down the corridor. As she breathed again, her thoughts took her back to the happy times they had enjoyed before the tragedy that was to overtake them.

Brian took hold of Stephanie's hands, as though to reassure himself that at least they still had each other. There was nothing he could say that would help. The months of waiting and trying to keep cheerful had taken their toll and now that the waiting was nearly over, neither of them dared to think ahead to the future in case their worst fears should be realised.

There were sounds of activity in the corridor outside again. The door opened... Stephanie and Brian anxiously searched the tired face of the man robed in white who came in, both longing, aching to find a clue to the answer to their unspoken query.

'You can come in now,' he said.
The two followed apprehensively to where a small child lay peacefully sleeping in his cot.

A hint of a smile flickered round the surgeon's face, over-riding the weariness and betraying a sense of relief and triumph.

'His new heart is working well,' he said, 'there is every reason to believe that he can make a full recovery.'

The child stirred and momentarily opened his eyes as he felt his mother gently tucking his teddy in beside him.

Lost in Arcadia

by

Nikki Perelandra

This bronzing body waits for the cloud to pass to be kissed again by the sun God. The heat soothes, burns, yet breezes play in long soft curls and tease the dancing, whirlwind doves. Blood and flame red geraniums shake in shallow terracotta pots. All basks and is healed and there is Ravelor Stravinsky and Daphnis or Apollo. He dreams of Satyrs and woods and rocks and pools with the Narcissus-like Daphnis. Always the heat and breezes shaking so roughly boughs of Laurel. Daphnis appears! A long legged boy, a crown of leaves on his brow, soft white toga, golden sandals with coiling straps up to his knees. He has eyes of azure and a scent of cinnamon, musk, incense. Where he walks, flowers grow...

The bronzing body rouses and with it the mind.

'What cost is my life?'

The friend, more Heathcliff than Daphnis appears with water from the spring. Clouds gather. A crow menaces - butterflies are blown off course. Why do the pigeons test their aerial agility? He hears a chord in arpeggio which he has not heard before - but it has gone, gone. But he wants it again and again - to deafen. The doves are pursuing the crow.

Heathcliff reminds Olaf that the Gathering takes place that night as it is the New Moon. It is to be in the ruined castle at the edge of the woods.

Olaf takes long in anxious preparation, choosing gentle adornments sometimes small flowers. Once he had used a thin liana of ivy to wind around and around his legs and body ending at a knot around his neck.

Torches lit the inside of the castle. There was mead to drink and many were already dancing to loud drum rhythms and discordant wind instruments. Occasionally a harpist would play and his friend would play a hammered dulcimer. Such beautiful interludes were all too brief before the pulsating of the drums returned.

Goran was there! He whom Olaf had yearned for, for several years. Tall and pale was Goran with yellow hair down his back. Pale, sky-blue eyes. He stood and looked restless as always. The diamond of his ear-ring picked up the light from the torch flames. Sparkling like a signal across the swaying bodies. Olaf had felt a surge of excitement at seeing him again but knew better than to speak. Olaf took a black candle and wrote in wax, 'Why not with me, Goran?' Goran left early, as always. Olaf watched him leave. Watched him take his horse from the stables and saw the light of the moon catch his hair and the mane and tail of his horse. Why did he always leave before the moon was at its zenith?

The next day Olaf was attending the class of the Spiritual Master with little Garadine sitting beside him. Garadine the dream! Croakey, desperate voice - hair as spiky as the mane of his roan pony. For some reason the Master named Garadine and a few others as not being allowed to progress. The lad took this very badly and whispered to Olaf, 'Why?'

'I know not,' replied Olaf, 'but you need not stay here at this level.'

The class dispersed and Olaf wondered what he was supposed to be progressing to, how and why.

Suddenly Garadine was by his side. 'Can I go with you?' he asked and Olaf noticed his tear stained cheeks. He looked so small and lost.

'Yes, of course, but quite where we go I do not know. Let my pony, Banba, take us away tonight.'

They mingled with the crowds on the outskirts of the school throughout the heat of the day and when the sun set they made their way to the grove where Banba the Grey was grazing. Garadine was delighted to be hauled up onto a bigger stronger pony than his own. He wore the short, thin brown robe of the orphans and when he was astride Banba his legs looked thin and white. Olaf sat behind him and realised he wanted to bite the back of the boy's neck. Banba walked on and her rhythmic gait eased them close together with her withers rising just at Garadine's thighs. Olaf had one hand on Banba's mane and the other around Garadine's waist. He could tell the boy was deliriously happy.

The moon was waxing and Banba picked her way carefully over the stony path. Garadine was getting sleepy for his head was lolling forward onto his chest. They were well away from the school now and seemed to be in a valley of trees and rocks.

Olaf wanted the boy and kissed the nape of his neck, very gently. Garadine's body stiffened, aroused from his reverie he said that he had to relieve himself. They stopped beside a moonlit pool beside which loomed a black rock. Garadine ran off into the shadows as Olaf let Banba drink from the pool. Olaf could see the lad climbing up the rock and when he was at the top he laughed and took off his robe.

74

'Olaf,' he cried, 'look at me!' He urinated into the pool - a silver, glistening arc. He teasingly put his robe on again, stretched his body then began the descent. He seemed to descend the rock on the far side for Olaf lost sight of him. All was quiet save the odd sound of a night bird and the water lapping around the rocks.

Olaf started clambering around the rock to where he thought the boy had been.

'Garadine. Garadine!'

'Dine, Dine, Dine...' came an echo.

Banba had followed Olaf, as she so often did, but the echo seemed to disturb her and as far as Olaf could make out, they were at the mouth of a vast cave. He called and again the echo and then silence.

Olaf stayed by the rock all night. Banba was calm and browsed.

The golden dawn revealed nothing. The cave was not as deep as Olaf had imagined and seemed to have no crevices. The sunlight arrived over the rocks and showed trees covered in yellow and white florets. Olaf began picking them and noticed what an intoxicating scent they had. He picked more and more and he began to feel giddy. He strew them around the mouth of the cave and onto the rock and floated some on the pool. He bent over the pool, cupped his hands and drank the cold water.

He drank and drank, far more than he needed to quench his thirst for somehow, in the water was the very essence of Garadine. He imagined he could taste him. Although he had always strived to quench his passion he now knew that if ever it were quenched that would be the end. The very end. He was doomed forever to wander these lands in search of love as he knew he had more love than anyone could take.

'Oh, Garadine,' he whispered into Banba's neck and wiped his tears on her mane.

Silence is Golden

by

Julian F Lannie

Dark clouds covered the night sky, a full moon peeked intermittently through the cracks, soon the rains would come. I had been sitting on my nerve ends for my courage to pick up these last three weeks. The first drops of rain fell onto the waiting ground, where the earth greedily drank them in. It was now or never. I had lived in this house for the past twenty years, all of them with my wife, she was gone now, well most of her!

Leaving the living room I went into the kitchen and opened the side door which led directly into the garage. Inside the cold damp garage I opened the boot of the car and watched as it rose silently. Leaning into the opening I took out my tool-box and assorted paraphernalia and stacked it onto the concrete floor, as I would need all the available space if I was only going to make one journey.

Coming back into the house I stood on the threshold and basked in the silence. I smiled at the lack of nagging that usually bounced around the house, the beautiful silence now devoid of the badgering and bitterness, it was finally over for me.

Back in the living room I felt a warmth embrace me as I looked out of the window at the rain cascading down outside. I was startled by the phone ringing and with a certain wariness I crossed the carpet and picked up the cream receiver (I had wanted a red one but she said it would clash with the curtains and as usual I timidly agreed).

'Hello....yes tomorrow at ten would be fine....thank-you, I certainly hope so...yes, yes things have been hectic...goodbye then.' I replaced the instrument and without further ado made my way upstairs. Entering the main bedroom I looked at the three full black heavy duty dustbin liners, their openings carefully taped up to avoid any spillage.

'Marjory had for the last eleven years of our marriage been a martyr to chocolate and her slim eight stone figure had exploded to nightmarish proportions. Her figure that had once been the envy of many of her friends and colleagues, was now that it had stabilised only the envy of the old Michelin man. That had all happened a long time before I decided to set out on my drastic but not totally unexpected course of action.

I laboured with the three heavy bags and with a shortage of breath and a shirt soaked in sweat I was able to shut up the boot of my car (I was already thinking in terms of mine and not ours, it felt good). Returning to the house I went from room to room turning off the lights, after doing this task I exited through the kitchen door and locked up behind me. Getting into the car I pressed the button on my key ring and the garage door slid silently sky-wards, the engine purred into life at the first turn of the ignition key, putting the car into first gear I drove slowly down the small drive and out into the street. Turning left I made my way cautiously down the electrically lit streets. The rain hammered relentlessly down as I picked my way down the carefully planned route.

I was into the city centre now, my concentrating on driving in an exemplary law abiding fashion. As I approached a set of traffic lights they turned from green to red, I slowed and stopped, a car pulled up alongside and I automatically turned my head, my heart did a somersault as I looked straight into the faces of two policemen, admittedly they weren't taking any notice of me but that didn't stop my hands from shaking and sweating as I gripped the steering wheel tightly. I stared intensely at the traffic lights willing them to change and to my surprise they did. The surprise caused my foot to slip off the clutch and after three or four kangaroo hops the engine stalled, the police car slid past and I saw that its occupants were both laughing, I felt like crying.

I managed to get the car started again and shot off like a scolded cat, ten minutes later and without any further mishaps I arrived at my destination. I parked the car and turned off the lights and the engine. I got out and locked up the car.

I was down by the river at a secluded spot, a footpath lay parallel to the bank and some sixty yards along the overgrown path a semi derelict shed stood at the bottom of a disused allotment.

I went along to the shed and with a stealth a guerilla engaged in jungle warfare would have been proud of checked that no-one was about, after convincing myself of that fact I entered the shed through the broken door and double checked inside, satisfied I returned to the car. I wished that I could have parked closer to the shed but realised that this was as good as I was going to get. I hauled one of the bags out of the boot and with the realisation that I was in for a back breaking time I set off. The awkward shape of the bag did little to help and upon reaching the shed my muscles were already aching and straining, the adrenalin was flowing and I fairly raced back to the car. I looked at my watch and saw that the trip had taken a scant five minutes to lose the first bag. I

shouldered the second liner and traipsed back down the pathway, sweat inter-
mingled with the rain as the exertions took their toll on my forty eight year old
body. The second bag joined the first and back at the car I saw that it had taken
me eleven minutes. The third journey took seventeen minutes as I had to stop
twice, such was the effort. All three bags were now covered with a mouldy tar-
paulin sheet that I had found in the shed.

The drive back home was uneventful and that night for the first time in many
weeks I slept soundly. The next morning I busied myself tidying up the house
in readiness for my guests. They arrived promptly on the stroke of ten, I offered them tea and they accepted that and my apologies for not being at home
for them over the past few days. We swapped small talk for twenty minutes
then I left them alone to get on with their chores. Thanks to this couple I would
be able to get away from this house inside the next week.

It was a month since I had put the house up for sale and after many protests
from the estate agents that I was seriously undervaluing the property my wishes
were granted and the offer was soon snapped up. The funds were being trans-
ferred the day after tomorrow into the new bank account I had set up at a different bank from the one I had used all my working life.

..... Three weeks after the man had left the house a tramp looking for a dry
place to lie his head stumbled across the shed and its contents, he ripped open
one of the bin liners and screamed.

At six o'clock the following evening the front door bell chimed at the mans
old home. Expecting friends both of the new owners went to the door, upon
opening it they were confronted by a woman of gargantuan stature who looked
as surprised as they were.

'What are you doing in my house?' She screeched at them.

'It's our house, what are you talking about?' The man answered but the large
woman took no notice of him and pushed her bulk past them and went into the
living room.

'Where's my furniture?' Her voice echoed round the room. She came out and
started for the stairs and began to mount them.

'Two months I've been away, looking after my sick mother and when I come
back there's strangers in my house.' A cry of where's my clothes bounded down
the stairs followed by her body. Tears were running down her cheeks.

'Wh, wh, where's my two lovely poodles?'

As the words left her mouth a tramp stepped into the hallway, he was carrying two dog collars, each engraved with a name and address.

78

Where News is Made

by

Sheila Barber

Pale and flabby compared with his former self, he had turned his back on city civilisation and now stepped carefully into the small rowing boat. He had had to talk so hard to persuade the fisherman to part with the boat for double its value that he was afraid to delay an instant; the old man urged by his comrades might even now change his mind. He could not understand why they insisted that no regular boat would be visiting the island. As far back as he could remember, the weekly steamer had not failed except in the great hurricane when he was only an infant. The sea looked calm and friendly, reflecting the brilliance of a radiant sky, so familiar, and at the same time made so unfamiliar by years spent in-land. He had to go back to the island. Nevertheless the anger and frustration which drove him to leave had never weakened, unlike the once sturdy, muscular limbs which had now to do their own driving. Never before had he been so aware of the brilliance of sunlight, the briny tang of sea, even the soft yielding of sand beneath his feet. A crab scuttling away reminded him of another shore where youngsters had once chased in joyful abandon, cooling themselves in never ending waves before flopping carelessly among weed and wavy sand heaps. He knew that, given youth over again, he would still leave, as certainly as he now sought to return. He flexed arms and legs, stretched, shook himself, for even in today's calm, the passage would challenge unpractised strength and concentration.

After a couple of minutes he relaxed in the once familiar rhythm of rowing as the craft responded to his clumsy pulling on the oars. For an instant he had thought the sea would reject him, frustrating his efforts to reach the island. Surely it could not grudge him his chance; he had had to leave. From the age of ten he had been an incipient news reporter. City cousins from the mainland had come for a holiday, scattering an amazing assortment of papers and magazines, which strangely had held little fascination for his brothers and sisters - only for him. He was designed to report news and the island made no news. Six years later he left. How beautiful the sea was! He felt he had never seen it so clearly, not in all the years of plunging in, playing with brothers, pulling fish triumphantly out.

Nothing happened on the island. Each day was the same - filled with sand and sun, food and fun. From a world of brothers and sisters, he had grown into the island's school world; other boys and girls now, steeper rocks to climb, longer hours of freedom. He could hardly wait to tussle again with his older brothers, roll on the beach with the younger ones. Mum and dad... he realised the boat was almost stationary, bobbing on the waves. This would not do! As he renewed his efforts with the oars refusing to admit tiredness he had never known, he thought of the years, ten whole years, he had been away. For ten years they had grown older - how would they be? He had had to go where new things happened but couldn't he have been back?

As arms bent and straightened, he felt sweat in every fold of his flesh. Why had he neglected to buy some simple shirts and shorts before he left the shore? City clothes clung to arms and legs, out of place on one who depended now on physical effort to reach shelter. Mentally he began to examine his appearance; from haircut to shoes he was out of place already. How foolish he would look to old companions! He remembered how silly they used to think the few visitors who would leave the steamer to holiday for a week until it returned to recall them to reality.

He kept watch on his newly-acquired compass, casting an eye towards clouds crossing the sky from the west. He must concentrate; to miss the island might seem ludicrous for a native but was he not now a novice? The men had seemed to warn him before he left. The old man had wanted him to give up, had kept insisting there would be no steamer. Why? All had seemed on the verge of saying more, and scrutinized him, and just repeated their warning not to row to the island. Could he have chosen the dark, mysterious depths for his destiny - please, not death yet.

Once a shark had appeared too close to his father's boat as they returned from fishing. He had stopped his two sons chattering so that he could pull harder, harder, harder. Clouds were increasing now and his pace was slowing. Careful to maintain rhythm, he began, pull by pull, to force the pace, scanning the horizon for first evidence of the island. He had no idea what distance he had rowed. The old days of racing another boat halfway round the island gave him no perspective now of time and distance, only a reminder of sums in the old classroom... and Mallie.

As the sky grew greyer and day drew nearer its end, he wondered if he could afford to think at all now of Mallie. When he left, it was without remorse. He was a news reporter and on the island there was no news. Girls in the city had gone out with him, had been a regular part of his life, wearing make-up, dancing and dining on the nights when he was not chasing news.

Muscles ached now, hands were sore, and sometimes oars lay sluggish in the surly sea, refusing to renew the rhythm essential to complete his chosen course. Mallie would tease him; she would not recognize the lad who had clambered up the face of the island's tallest cliff. Until his fourteenth birthday that cliff had lorded it over all. The toughest were resigned to approach only from gentler slopes behind. First to applaud his unique conquest had been thin, boyish Mallie, hair flying wildly. She had always romped with the lads but that day he had touched her body, even pressed trembling lips to her face. His mind must direct the boat not his dreams; press his arms to greater effort, not revert to days of play and pleasure.

Panic threatened; the boat was tossing of its own accord as he forgot to attend to its direction. Hastily checking his compass again, he knew exhaustion as never before: slowly tired arms took control of reluctant oars. Eyes searched in growing desperation; somewhere across the water was the island, and Mallie; he refused to know the passing years. Only the recognition of a crest of trees, appearing and reappearing, told his mind to urge his arms. Like a car ready for the rust heap, slowing as it reaches the top of a hill, so his boat reached shore. In anger and agony he stepped again onto the now darkened island. Shaking with weariness and anticipation, he surveyed the empty beach, his ears hearing the human silence - only curlews cried. He had never known the beach unpeopled, an arrival unacclaimed.

Morning brought revelation. A few bodies sat or lay in huts; most had been conscientiously carried, or dragged, to the Great Cave of Ancestors. One or two had been dropped on the path, their carriers sprawled on top. No one lived. Only a rare eruption of Rupa or the more probable coming of hurricane Hannah would conclude the contagion. He had come back, and the island had made news.

Saint Ethelbert

by

Sydney Kent

Martyrs are usually well known, at least in the locality of their martyrdom. Not so St Ethelbert, who being slain in the depths of tranquil Herefordshire, is today almost completely forgotten. The murder of Ethelbert on the night of May 20th/21st 794 AD. was an important influence on English history. It was the trigger event which started the rapid decline in the power and prosperity of the Kingdom of Mercia.

Offa began his rule in 755 AD. and under him Mercia developed into the largest and most powerful kingdom in England, absorbing several smaller kingdoms. It eventually stretched from the borders of Wales to East Anglia. Offas capital was Tamworth and his chief bishopric, Lichfield, was independent of Canterbury.

Offa was renowned for driving back the Welsh and subsequently building his Dyke during 782-783 AD. to define the border between Mercia and the kingdoms of the Welsh princes. In addition to the powerful defence of his kingdom Offa encouraged learning and laid down many laws for the wise government of his subjects. Offa had carefully strengthened his links with the West Saxons by marrying his elder daughter Eadburth to Beorhtric King of Wessex. He had also promised his youngest daughter Elfrida, to Ethelbert son of King Ethelred of the East Angles again with the idea of further strengthening his kingdom.

The young couple had known each other since childhood, Offa and his wife Quendrida had visited Ethelred and his Queen Leofruna at their castle at Bury St Edmunds on several occasions. During one of those visits and without her husbands knowledge Quendrida had tried to seduce Ethelbert who was tall, handsome and an extremely good horseman. However Ethelbert who had received a religious upbringing, scorned her advances much to her bitter disappointment. Quendrida noted for having a smooth tongue and a wicked heart vowed to revenge the rebuttal.

Ethelbert succeeded his father Ethelred as King of the East Angles. Both were reputed to be very good kings much loved and respected by their subjects. After the period of mourning was over Ethelbert decided that he ought to marry. His thoughts turned to Elfrida who had been promised to him some time previously. He sent messengers to Offa to remind him of his promise. When the messengers returned they told Ethelbert that Offa wished the wedding to go ahead.

Offa was delighted with the idea that Ethelbert was to marry his daughter, this he felt could lead to the peaceful unification of the two kingdoms. Accordingly he invited Ethelbert to his hill top castle, at Sutton Walls, built on the site of both an Iron Age Fort and a Roman encampment which overlooked the valley of the River Lugg. The wedding ceremony was to be performed by Ealdwulf the Archbishop of Lichfield.

Quendrida loathed the idea of her daughter being married to Ethelbert who had previously refused her advances, and plotted to have him killed before the wedding could take place. She tried to talk Offa into carrying out the murder himself by trying to persuade him that Ethelbert's real intention was to take over Mercia and depose him. However Offa refused to listen to her treachery.

Ethelbert planned to journey to Hereford accompanied by a number of his Alderman and Thanes. The night before his departure, his Mother Leofruna had a nightmare and did not want her son to go. As the party were about to leave the ground shook, the sky became very dark and there was a violent thunder storm. Many of the party were afraid but Ethelbert said 'let us do what is expedient, let us humble ourselves before God and prostrate on the ground, let us ask the Lord to remove from our hearts and bodies the darkness and pour into us the light of his brightness.' All bowed to the ground as Ethelbert prayed and the sun suddenly shone out.

Several times during the journey the party were subjected to further storms which worried many of the travellers, however Ethelbert comforted those who were disturbed by the bad weather. The wedding party eventually arrived at the River Severn which they crossed at Worcester, travelling on via the Malvern Hills to Hereford where they camped whilst Ambassadors were sent to inform Offa of their arrival.

Whilst Ethelbert waited for the Ambassadors to return he sat by the River Wye and dozed. He dreamt that the roof of his palace had tumbled down, and that the corners of the bridal bed had been torn off. He had a vision of his Mother weeping tears of blood and saw a beautiful tree growing in his palace, at the roots were men steadily cutting, and a torrent of blood flowed out towards the east. He saw a column of light brighter than the sun with a vision of an angel carrying a chalice of blood which it sprinkled onto a little wooden church which then grew into a great stone church filled with a large singing congregation. His advisers interpreted the dream to mean that he would attain greater powers and excellence than former kings.

The Ambassadors were gladly received by King Offa but not by Quendrida who was extremely bitter that her youngest daughter was to marry Ethelbert. Because Offa still refused to kill Ethelbert she schemed herself to do the dreadful deed. She turned to Offa's chief servant Gymbert who had fought in many battles alongside his Master. Gymbert was the Warder of the castle holding the keys to its every door, and the executioner when need arose. Quendrida promised Gymbert his freedom if he could kill Ethelbert. The plan she cunningly plotted was for Ethelbert to be given a bedroom over a cellar passageway, Gymbert was to devise and fit a wooden trap door in the floor which could be lowered below at the appropriate time.

There was a great welcoming feast in the castle when Ethelbert and his party arrived, a great deal of wine was drunk and Quendrida made sure Offa drank excessively so that she could once more try to convince him to kill the visiting King.

The following day, the 20th of May 794, was the eve of the wedding, most of the nobles went out hunting whilst Ethelbert and Elfrida remained at the Castle and walked in the surrounding woods planning for their return to Ethelbert's castle at Bury St Edmunds.

That night there was much feasting and merriment after all the nobles returned from the hunt. Quendridas plan went into action. Ethelbert was given drugged wine during the evening and when he retired to his bedroom he sent all his servants away before he collapsed in a drunken stupor on to a chair which had previously been carefully placed on top of the trapdoor.

When they were sure Ethelbert was completely unconscious Gymbert and his men slowly lowered the trap door with the sleeping victim into the passage below to where they were waiting. Gymbert reached for his sword only to find that he had accidently discarded it during the earlier feasting. He grabbed the victims own sword and with one savage blow decapitated the hapless Ethelbert. Gymbert and his men then furtively carried off the body through the back gate of the castle where they put it on to a cart. They set off towards the River Lugg intending to throw the body into the river, however part way there they remembered that Quendrida had instructed that the body should be buried. Close to the river they dug a pit and cast in both the body and the head before fleeing.

Like many historical tales there are two versions of the slaying, both agree on the circumstances just vary in the detail. The alternative is that it was thought that Queen Quendrida did in fact persuade Offa to arrange the murder of Ethelbert. This he achieved by bribing one of his men Winebert to carry out the foul deed. Winebert knew Ethelbert well as he had been raised in the house of his father King Ethelred. When Ethelbert arrived at Sutton he was persuaded by Winebert to give him his sword and during a private audience with Offa Winebert rushed him and beheaded the defenceless Ethelbert with his own sword. The body was then dropped through a trap door to the cellar below, before it was taken and buried by the river.

When the news of the horrific murder spread through the castle Ethelbert's servants fled fearful that they would meet the same fate. Offa was extremely distressed. Elfrida was so upset by the murder of her bridegroom on their wedding eve that she immediately left the castle and joined a small convent of nuns in Lincolnshire.

After three days mourning Offa emerged from his chamber and sent an army to Ethelbert's kingdom fearful that the East Angles would attack him and Mercia in retaliation for the murder of their beloved King. Ealdwulf, the Archbishop of Lichfield remonstrated with Offa and persuaded him to search for the body of Ethelbert so it might be buried properly in the little church of the blessed Virgin Mary at Hereford.

Towards evening on the following day the searchers came to the bank of the River Lugg at Marden, as they were about to call off their search for the day a beam of light streamed down and rested on to a spot close to the river. The searchers dug and found the body and head separately wrapped in a cloak. They borrowed a cart from a farm nearby and set off for the drive into Hereford. When the body was removed from the ground a spring gushed forth which was later claimed to possess healing powers particularly for curing eye problems.

On the journey to Hereford the party stopped at nightfall. In the morning before they set off again they realised that the head had fallen from the cart. They carefully retraced their steps and found a man leaping and shouting for joy. He told them that he was a blind man who lived in Marden and that he had stumbled over something in the roadway which he had picked up. As he touched it his blindness was cured. He then found that the thing he had stumbled over was a severed head.

The searchers reclaimed the head and continued their journey to Hereford. On the way they paused at a spot near to what was to be the final resting place of the body, and a spring gushed forth here also. This conduit can still be found at the corner of Castle Green near Hereford cathedral, its water is claimed to be good for ulcers and sores. There were soon reports of many wonderful miracles of healing happening at the tomb.

When Offa heard of these miracles he journeyed to Rome to make his confession before Pope Adrian who directed him to build a church at Marden where Ethelbert's body had been first buried and a minster of stone in place of the church which was his final resting place, and decreed it was to be dedicated to the Blessed Virgin Mary and Saint Ethelbert.

King Offa lived for less than two years after Ethelberts murder, and the whole of that the time he spent in atonement for the great sin he had allowed to be committed. He also founded a Monastery at St Albans and churches at Bath, Offley (Hertfordshire) and Winchcombe (Gloucestershire). He was buried just outside Bedford in a small chapel, however one time the River Ouse flooded and washed away both the chapel and the bones of King Offa. Offa's only son Ecgfdrith who had been effectively ruling Mercia since the murder of Ethelbert survived his father by 141 days.

St Ethelberts Well at Marden is situated inside the rear of the Parish Church of St Mary the Virgin. In the west wall near the well is a niche which originally contained an effigy of St Ethelbert but is now just used as a cupboard. The coat of arms assigned to St Ethelbert in the middle ages were painted on the west wall but covered over in 1763 when the church was whitewashed. On either side of the south door into the church are carved in stone the heads of St Ethelbert and Pope Adrian.

All for One ... One for all

by

Catherine Wells

The warm sun gleamed onto the cats' furry backs, making them 'shine in their glory' Ned had said. Lolly, with his black velvet coat and bright yellow-green eyes, then Henry, with his clean white coat and ginger patches, and Tiger, the grey long-haired tabby with piercing sun-yellow eyes, who loved to wrap himself around Ned's shoulders.

Lily had looked forward to her husband's retirement. He had worked long hours at the shop. They had both worked hard at what had seemed, lately, to be a never-ending round of worrying, niggling jobs - feeding the animals, checking them all, checking the stock, trying to be sure the animals went to decent homes. Decent homes? How could they tell if a home was 'decent' enough? People put on such faces and such pretences to buy a pet, then could just the same forget about it in a few months.

She had long since wanted Ned to sell up and retire, but he kept finding excuses. Then Lily was ill that winter, and soon after Ned, with 'flu, then chest troubles, then the shop could not look after itself. After that, Lily did not have to pressure her husband - he was relieved when the estate agent told them they had an interested buyer, and in a month it was all settled. They had a good price for the shop, and for the 'good will', and the young couple who were taking it seemed like a caring pair - full of good intentions, eager to make improvements and changes. That was their concern - all she wanted was to have some time to themselves, to look after Ned, and to sometimes be looked after.

They bought a small cottage, with a manageable garden back and front - a change indeed, to the flat above the shop, which had been cosy, but there was always the business and other things to worry about all the time. Ned had decided to take the three cats with them to the new home. Lily would have been happy to have left them in the care of the young couple who were eager to look after them if they could not find homes for them all. The cats had been at the shop since they were kittens and had not been lucky enough to have been found owners before they sold up, and somehow, Ned felt they were his responsibility. Ned has his way, and the cats went with them to their new home - 'good mousers' Ned had said, 'clever clean creatures'. Lily liked the garden in the new place, but she did not want to garden in it alone. She looked forward to Ned having the time now to spend a few hours in it with her, but he seemed to be fussing over those cats like they were children. He had taken to staying for hours in the timber shed at the bottom of the back garden - not that he was alone, as the cats never left him for a minute. They followed him everywhere, and just when Lily thought Ned wanted her company, they would lie all over him like a winter coat. He had made them all a long seat with a cosy blanket on it, in the sunny end of the shed, and Lily thought they looked like four dozing statues, as she peered in through the window.

Lily liked animals, but the cats were taking too much of Ned, and Ned was letting them. He spent so much time talking to them, stroking them, grooming them, and then there was the feeding. The feeding she resented most. Ned would slowly cut up little delicacies for them, and would then watch them intently, as they ate side by side, from their three china bowls. She did not deny that she felt a certain pleasure from them, but they did not seem to want her, only Ned. He seemed to derive so much private pleasure and contentment from preparing their meals - much more, she thought, than making her a cup of tea. How many hours had she spent whilst lovingly cooking his meals? Countless, over the years, she thought, and now he could not spare a few special hours with her. Wherever Ned went, his three loyal comrades went, too, and Ned's attention never left them. He had made them three baskets which he'd put in she and Ned's bedroom - not that they stayed in them to sleep for long, she thought. Lily would feel their substantial weights on their bed most nights - one in the middle, one over by Ned's side, and the other wrapped around his neck like a casually arranged scarf. How Ned seemed to get a comfortable night's sleep she could not imagine, as her own body was beginning to complain at the unnatural cramping it was put through. She was a reasonable person, she thought, and so was Ned - when he was not besotted. Her attempts at trying to have a rational talk with Ned had not been very productive. His suggestions that she try and 'get out a bit more, and to 'make some friends of her own' was not remotely what Lily wanted to hear. Lily could not, would not, think of harming the cats. She respected them in their own place, but she resented, increasingly, their complete 'takeover' of her husband. It was not in her nature to harm any living creature, in fact, she had even considered having an animal of her own, though not a cat, a dog perhaps, to put their noses 'out of joint' a little - but she had a sneaking feeling that it, too, would join the felines in their admiration for Ned, and so leave her feeling more out in the cold than ever. She watched the four of them - Ned, with his strong square jawline and steel-blue eyes: the cat Lolly rolling in ecstasies at the sight of him. The cat Henry, getting bigger now with his ginger patches expanding as a result of the tasty meals Ned gave him. The cat Tiger, whose only resemblance, Lily thought, to his name, were his stripes - the rest of him was sloppy soft and fat. She watched resentfully, as Ned once again prepared some minced delicacy for their midday meal: the cats rolling and rubbing in eager anticipation. She saw how careful Ned was to scrape every little bit into their dishes, and when it was time for a tinned meal he would ensure that the tin was scraped so clean - giving each cat, in turn, a taste of it from his finger, until the inside of the tin was finally clean.

It was a Tuesday afternoon and Lily began to realise that she did not like, anymore, the planning of a meal for Ned, let alone the cooking of it. She had always enjoyed her creative feelings, her culinary abilities, until Ned had become so engrossed with the cats. He no longer gave her compliments on her efforts, so she felt that she did not want to make an effort. She looked at the clock on the wooden polished side-board in the dining-room of their cottage. It was half- past three in the afternoon. Ned was outside in the timber shed he shared with his cats, and they were all dozing with noises of snoring and purring alternating with each other.

Lily knew that she did not feel like making the efforts to cook at all, yet she knew, too, that it was not in her nature to see Ned suffer by not feeding him. She looked dismally into the shelves of the neatly arranged pantry. On Tuesdays she had always faithfully cooked Ned a shepherd's pie. Today she had not even thought to go to the butcher's for the lean minced beef that she always bought. Three of the six pantry shelves were filled with tins of the very best cat meat - beef, fish, chicken - all neatly stacked and arranged by Ned so that he would never have to served the same tin of food for two consecutive days. Ned always made sure that there were enough tins for a few weeks' supply in case of emergencies, he had said. As she sliced up the onions and peeled the potatoes for the shepherd's pie she looked at the tin in her hand.

'Super-tasty Beef Treat for cats that know the best'. She opened the tin and it looked appetising and did, indeed, smell of fresh beef. Ned would appreciate the extra amount he would get too, as it was a large tin. There was more meat in one of the tins he bought for those cats than ever she could afford to buy for them on a Tuesday.

She lovingly rubbed the inside of the tin with her finger just as Ned did, until it was shining clean inside, and made sure every morsel went into the pie. Ned would only get the best. The pie smelled quite delicious with the onions and creamy mashed potatoes, as it went on browning in the oven.

Lily sat down with a pleasant glow of satisfaction after washing the dinner-plates. Three cats oozed contentment and were lying all over Ned, after he had fed them their Tuesday tin of Beef Treat. Ned looked puzzled as he had wondered why one tin was missing on the second shelf - 'not like me' - he had said, whilst welcoming the diversion of a cat rubbing his ankle. Ned complimented his wife on 'the best shepherd's pie for many a while', and he added that now she had changed the recipe she ought to 'stick to this one'. Lily was sure that he meant every word. She looked bemused at her husband - she could not foresee any real difficulty in her doing that as long as Ned did not bother himself too much about the pantry shelves, for after all, if she was not sure she could beat them or join them, she most certainly could see that they were all treated the same...

Man of Incredible Wealth

by

Basil Woods

'Bloody Harold Wilson. Who the hell does he think he is? Destroying my business; running little old Ireland's precious industry. I'm not standing for it; not in 1964 I'm not, not ever, I tell you ....'

The crimson faced, diminutive man in the American-cut, silver-grey seersucker suit and emerald green bow-tie, paused for breath. If ever there was a sorely aggrieved man here, undebatably, was one. He was beside himself with uncontainable rage.

Normally an oasis where conversation was tacitly reduced to the lower ranges of decibels, the elegant resident's lounge of Dublin's Shelbourne Hotel was the last place in the world where one one would expect to be disturbed by a fracas. After a frustrating, fog-diverted journey I had booked in at the Shelbourne intending to have a quiet meal and an early bed. At the last moment my resolution wilted and I allowed the waiter to steer me towards the lounge with the promise of black coffee and a night-cap of Baileys Original. Entering the room and hearing the racket I turned to beat a retreat. But it was too late: the chance of recruiting an addition to his captive audience was not going to be passed up by the irate Irishman.

'I'll fix the sod,' he screamed warming to his theme. 'He'll soon find out that I can't be trifled with. *Me, a man of incredible wealth and influence.*' He stopped and threw a challenging look at his captives. There were five of us : a lugubrious clerical gentleman; a self-conscious Civil Servant accompanied by a petite blonde who looked too young to be his wife; a bespectacled, silver-haired maiden lady busily clicking her knitting needles, and myself. We shared a common emotion - speechless astonishment!

He must have judged that I was the most gullible victim of the five. Fastening me with an accusatory stare, he barked: 'Do you know who I was with this *very* afternoon?'

There was no need for me to answer; the monologue continued unstoppably.

'With my friend the Taoiseach, Ireland's Prime Minister!'

Not one of us had the nerve to interject. For my part, I was still trying to decide whether he was touched, a drunk or an out-and-out chancer.

91

To look at he didn't appear to be under the influence, nor mentally disturbed for that matter. A small cock-sparrow of a man, his spiky reddish hair brushed forward to cover a balding forehead, the excitable Irishman might have passed unnoticed but for a pair of penetrating, bright blue eyes, out of which he regarded his fellow humans with unyielding suspicion. A phoney, I concluded - perhaps a professional confidence trickster?

The waiter arrived with coffee and liqueur, and a double whiskey for the Irishman which he lowered in a single gulp, making me wonder whether the earlier diagnosis of his condition was right. If anything, it heightened his sense of injustice and loosened his tongue still further.

'Call himself British Prime Minister, the man's an idiot. Surely one of his over paid officials could tell him that sticking on an import surcharge is bloody madness. It's illegal, it's indecent, it's immoral!'

He was getting really worked up and, with barely a pause for breath, went on: Here I am, owning over a hundred factories throughout the world, six in bloody England, and this clown comes along and slaps fifteen percent surcharge on everything we bring into the country. Hundreds of people, thousands more like it, are going to lose their jobs, and all thanks to Mr Bloody Harold Wilson, that madman, wicked charlatan...' his voice trailed off.

The clergyman, quick to see his opportunity, mumbled something about having to prepare a sermon and shuffled out of the room without a backward glance. The loss of one member of the captive audience seemed to act as a challenge, and the Irishman returned to the attack concentrating his verbal assault on me.

'Well, that silly bastard is going to be taught a lesson he won't forget easily. he can't muck me around. He'll find out that I am *a man of incredible wealth and influence.* I have lots of good friends in high places. Do you know who I will be staying with in a few weeks time?' He glared at me, adding with a triumphant smirk: 'With the President of the United States and his family at their ranch in Texas!'

Misguidedly, I attempted to change the subject by commenting approvingly on his expensive looking tan. I regretted it instantly. It merely stirred him to greater heights of fantasy.

'Just got back from a week's cruise on the Med on my old friend Onassis's yacht,' he declared airily. 'Super time, lovely people,' he continued.

'Now, there's a big league hitter for you - Aristotle Onassis, richest man in the world. His lovely new wife, Jackie, was there, too. So were lots of other high powered folks. These people - all my dear friends - will be rooting for me.

Just wait until that little skunk in Whitehall, and his miserable government, hear from them about the criminal thing that's been done to me. That bunch of smart-arses in Downing Street won't know what's hit them.' He finished flushed with triumph.

By this time I was becoming increasingly restive. So were the remaining occupants of the residents lounge, now reduced to the middle aged man and his paramour, who presently got up, excused themselves briefly and disappeared, no doubt to more interesting pursuits than listening to the loud mouthed rantings of an Irish bore. He was not going to let me escape, however. Signalling to the waiter to bring another round of drinks he continued his verbal assault, brushing aside my feeble attempts to explain that I didn't want another drink and had to get up early in the morning.

He fiddled in his breast pocket pulling out a wallet. I wondered anxiously what the next great revelation would be. Extracting a US dollar bill from a fat bankroll, he thrust it in front of my eyes.

'Do you recognise that signature?' he demanded. I studied the note closely. Above the facsimile of the US Secretary of the Treasury's name, scrawled in purple ink, was what appeared to be an identical signature: 'Douglas Dillon'. Before I could express surprise or mystification he announced, with obvious pride, that it had been given to him as a 'memento from my old friend Duggie Dillon'. Then, seeing my look of utter incredulity he delivered the ultimate block-buster: 'As a matter of fact,' he declared nonchantly, 'I've got his wife upstairs with me now!'

I knew then that I had neither a drunk nor a chancer, but a nut-case on my hands!

Throwing normal courtesies overboard, I mumbled that I needed a pee urgently and vanished from the room.

Some weeks later, at the end of the arduous business trip that had started unexpectedly in Dublin and proceeded eventually via New York to the Mid-West, I was holed up in one of those soulless hotels at Chicaigo's O'Hare airport waiting for a much delayed connecting flight back to London. It had been a tough and not altogether successful negotiation. I was feeling jaded and anxious to be safely on my way home. As usual, I couldn't sleep in the over heated, over-purified atmosphere that the average American hotel seems to regard as a biological necessity of *homo sapiens* . Scrolling through the score of TV channels, I searched in vain for something of interest to anyone with an IQ of even the most modest dimensions. Finally, I settled for a newscast sandwiched in between a feast of tasteless junk food commercials. One item held my attention momentarily. It showed the American President - that great gangling Texan chap with a ten-gallon hat permanently on his head (Lyndon Johnson, wasn't it?) entertaining 'good friends and neighbours' at his million dollar ranch somewhere in the Deep South.

I was just about to switch the set off and make another futile attempt at sleep when the cameraman panned in on one of the guests walking, arm-in-arm, with the President's wife and evidently holding her in intensely animated, one-sided conversation. 'With the First Lady,' the American telecaster's voice droned on, 'is one of the President's best friends from across the water, the billionaire Irish businessman Mr....' Indeed it was true, for their on the silver screen was the never- to-be, forgotten cock-sparrow figure of .... you've guessed it, *the man of incredible wealth and influence!*

Josey

by

Ray Moore

'Josey! Come here girl and read this,' came the old voice from the trailer.

'Comin', Gran, da.' Josey pulled up her sock and skipped one skip to the caravan door.

'What it it?' she asked, climbing the step to enter the trailer.

The old man with the rock-stone voice sat at a pull down table polishing an ornamental brass Dray horse.

'This,' he said, flicking an envelope across the table towards her. 'Read it for me girl. And no joshin' me.'

'I won't josh ya Gran, da, if you speaks English for the whole day.'

'And I tell you girl, I tell you this,' growled the old man, shaking the grime stained rag in his hand. 'Who do ya think you are, the Romany princess of Durndow Common?'

Josey curtseyed and pulled up her other sock. 'Well, if you's the king of Gypsies - must make me a princess,' she said, and twisted her mouth to a false smile.

'You's no princess, you're a little mumper and a cheeky little mare. Just like your mother. And if ever she spoke to me like you - well, I'll tell you,' boomed the old man, raising a fist.

'And you just an old crank, with more holes in your vest than an inside-out hedgehog,' retorted Josey, sticking out her tongue.

The old man slid from behind the table with a speed, that in his young days, had left many an opponent wondering which world they were in. His huge hands cocked under Josey's arms as he lifted her in to the air.

She seemed to float in mid-air in the moment before the power of the old man's lift gave in to the force of gravity.

'Gran, da. Gran, da,' she squealed.

The old man caught her on the way down and hugged her to his chest. He kissed her head, her forehead, her hand and blew roughly into her neck.

Josey squeaked and threw her skinny arms around him.

The old man danced a jig and care and time stopped for another precious moment, in his mind.

95

'Come on, sit at the table with me and tell me all that ails ya.'

'Nothin' ails me, Gran, da - only.'

'Only what, girl?'

'Only - why don't you like to talk the English?'

'And what, madam, do I talk?' he said gently, as he shuffled his way along the seat to make room for her.

Josey glanced at the letter and ignored it.

'But Gran, da, when I used to talk the Romany at school, them other kids they'd take the rise.'

'And?' said the old man, turning the Dray Horse slowly.

'And I don't want to be called a Gypsy.'

'But that's what you are my flower petal. And proud as anyone you should be.'

'Liked is what I want to be, Gran, da. All them other kids, they hate me.'

'They's only dry-bread Gawjos,' said the old man, anger in his voice. 'They hate everyone that's not like them. Half the time they hates themselves, Josey. Don't take no notice of them! Remember, we've been a part of life around here for a lot longer than quite a few of those townies as likes to call themselves villagers now.'

Josey moved along the seat and leaned against her Grandfather. 'How can I not take notice of them? We live with them now.'

The old man stared silently at the letter. 'One day, Josey, we'll move on. We only live with them for the moment, while there's hops to pick.'

'I don't remember living anywhere else, Gran, da. And Daddy says that everyone drinks lager nowadays and the Hops won't be needed in the future. Is that why we have lived here all the time, Gran, da, 'cause everyone drinks lager?'

'No, no, no. We've been comin' here since I was a chavvie like yourself. Sometimes then we would stay more than the Hop season. I remember when they built that new housing estate beyond the village we were here for four years there was so much work.'

'But I'm nine, Gran, da. And there's only an old housing estate beyond the village now.'

Slapping his hand on the table the old man began to laugh. He laughed till the button on his pants gave way to his stomach.

Josey started to laugh along with him. 'What are you laughing about Gran,da? Gran, da, what are you laughing about?'

'Oh, it doesn't matter, girl.' He stopped abruptly, lowering his eyes to his hands. 'There's no school in the world that could teach your kind of reasoning. No, not even a Gawjo school.'

'Daddy says that the village school is the best for miles around.'

'Ah, Josey, take no notice of him,' bellowed the old man.' He's only a hedge-humper, never should have let him marry your mother.'

Josey looked down. 'I wouldn't be here if he hadn't though. Gran,da.'

'How do you know that,' snapped the old man, scowling.

'I do know where we really come form, Gran, da. We's told them things at school.'

'What! At your age? Ha, pity they don't teach you about the real world.'

'Like how to collect the scrap and make pegs from branches,' said Josey.' And walk for miles through the snow in winter to sell painted fir twigs at Christmas?'

The old man sighed. 'There's always a price for everything, Josey. And those old days ... We were free, Josey.'

'I'd like to go to the lavvy when I felt like it. Not have to go behind hedges or wait till no one is comin,' said Josey. 'I'd like a toilet like they've got at school. If we moved on to that site they've got for us down the road we'd have a proper toilet. That's free.'

'Free is it?' said the old man, distantly.' No scrap no more, all recycled,' he went on. 'Used to be a time when I could make a months money in a couple of days. Everybody got these parts and labour guarantee things nowadays. Makes things last longer. All wised up most people now. Even the big shops. Take all the old stuff when they deliver a new washer or cooker. Was a time when you could find easy money round the builder. Caught on to that though eventually. Do you know, Josey, the last time I went on a building site and asked to scrat around for scrap, the foreman took me to a small compound and showed me a skip full near to the top with bits of lead and copper and brass, 'Look at that skip,' he said 'When that's full it will pay for the lad's Christmas do and take us all on holiday, with money in kitty to spend,' That's what we're dealing with today, Josey. - Bloody Gawjos.'

Josey stood on the seat and gave him a hug. 'Don't worry Gran, da, my teacher says I'm bright. I'll look after you when I'm older, Gran, da. Don't worry.'

'Yes, Josey,' said the old man. 'You're bright alright. The brightest star that ever shone in my life.' The old man continued, 'I remember the first time I set eyes on your Grandma. Her family moved up here from Kent. Nine years old we was, the both of us. And I loved her from the first moment I saw her. I love her still, though she's gone. And you, Josey, you's her all over again. And as long as we have people like you we will never really be caged, Josey. Maybe a part of the old times will never die.'

Picking up the letter the old man opened it. 'Here, girl, use what they've taught you ya' tell me what it says.'

She took the piece of paper and began to read, 'Dear Mr Smith, With regard to your impending move and eligibility for the Community Charge....'

Accidents Will Happen

by

Diane Loxton

Janet Harper sat back and skimmed over the page she'd just written. The first few lines she thought, were always the worst. Peeling the ideas from your mind and placing them onto a clean sheet of paper was difficult, but a challenge she enjoyed. This piece was proving more difficult than she'd imagined. A woman's magazine was running a 'writer of the year' competition with a considerable amount of money for the winner, but more importantly to Janet was the recognition that winning would bring.

At 39, Janet wanted, indeed needed to be recognised in her own right. Her young family, though growing rapidly wasn't enough for her, she'd realised that when Adam and Katrin had started school together almost seven years ago, with Alan out at work all day, Janet had had lots of time to sit and ponder as to where her life was going, that was when she'd taken up writing. It was just a pity that she couldn't come up with an idea for this particular story.

The door opened behind her, and she heard the excited voices of her children, 'it can't be that time already' she muttered glancing at the clock, which confirmed it was indeed 4.30. Alan would be home in less than an hour, and here she was sat over her books, with all her paraphernalia strewn across the dining table, and tea not even started! She grimaced when she recalled the last time she'd forgotten the time, she'd gotten so absorbed in her work. The car had been hers for the day on condition that she pick the children up from school, and Alan from work, by the time she got round to Alan he'd been literally jumping up and down, his sarcastic remarks still burned in her ears.

'Why can't you do something worthwhile with you're time, or else find a job?' he'd whined. Alan treated her writing as a tiresome child, it was to be endured, a fanciful hobby, nothing more. He didn't appreciate how difficult it was to get work into print, although she had done it, once, and only a short story at that, but nevertheless it had put her on a high, and from that moment on she'd been hooked. The cheque received for the article had been small, she recalled that Alan hadn't complained when she'd handed it over to him to spend.

Janet pushed all thoughts of writing from her mind, and concentrated on clearing the table and cooking the tea. She'd literally just finished dishing up

99

when Alan arrived. His sardonic smile was enough to tell her he'd already guessed how she'd spent her day.

They ate in a sombre mood, the children occasionally breaking the silence with whispers of some shared conspiracy. Janet cleared the dishes while the kids watched TV and Alan read the paper. She joined them for an hour, then ushered the children up to their rooms to do homework. She helped Katrin with her maths, and checked over Adam's spelling before returning to the sitting room.

Alan was watching some game show when she came downstairs.

'How was your day?' she asked hoping to break the silence and clear some of the tension she felt building,

'More to the point how was yours? I see you've been sat down for most of it,' his tone warned her she was walking on thin ice.

'It's for that competition in the magazine I told you about.'

'More drivel, for bored housewives to read I suppose.'

That was typical of him, she wondered if other woman had to suffer this sort of punishment each time they did something they enjoyed.

Fearing a head on confrontation, Janet went and busied herself in the kitchen, re-appearing half an hour later with a steaming mug of coffee for him, only to find Alan asleep on the sofa. Straightening the living room and switching off the TV, Janet decided to have a bath, a long soak would do her the world of good and early night wouldn't go amiss either.

Relaxing in the bath, Janet's thoughts turned to Alan, and his resentment of her writing. It seemed to her that he was jealous of any ability she possessed and he didn't. If lunch was a success Alan would find some small defect, real or imagined to mar her enjoyment. One year she'd decorated the bathroom, and tiled it all by herself, expecting gratitude for saving him effort, or even warm praise, she'd found herself severely disappointed. Alan noticed only the wrinkles in the not yet dry wallpaper, 'If you'd have waited until the weekend, I could've done it properly', the look, the tone of voice he so often used on her was one that Janet had learned to anticipate after sixteen years of marriage.

'Perhaps he hates me,' the thought came so easily it shocked her. 'I'm getting paranoid,' she thought to herself, 'of course he doesn't hate me,' but the seed had been planted, the doubt began to grow.

Over the next few days Janet began to see her husband in a different light, began to see a stranger emerge from the shell of the man she married. Every comment he made seemed to be loaded with veiled criticism aimed at her. When they'd first got married, Alan had cherished her. His smile had been quick, his laughter real, and the words 'I love you' never far from his lips. When was the last time Alan had spoken those words to her with any real meaning? Just when had Alan changed into this cold critical stranger? The doubt turned into certainty, Alan didn't love her anymore. The statement was out, she accepted it quite calmly, 'He can't hurt me anymore' she spoke the words softly, with relief.

Over the proceeding weeks the initial numbness Janet had felt began to wear off, and a new unexpected feeling of contempt began to emerge. Alan had no idea of Janet's feelings for him, of course he'd noticed a new coldness in her eyes whenever he approached her in bed, and he'd put it down to her age and possibly the approaching menopause, didn't all women get a little cranky at his wife's time of life? He guessed she might be having problems with this latest attempt of a story, but she should pull herself together and not take it out on him, after all it was only a hobby, not a career for Christ's sake!

Arriving home on a cold wet miserable Monday, Alan Harper was not in the best of moods. His mood was not lightened when he walked into the house and found Janet sat down at the dining table with her head buried in yet another book

'Where are the kids?' he asked noticing the edge in his voice.

'Upstairs doing homework I think.'

'Have they eaten?'

'No,' - a simple answer that unleashed a torrent of anger that until then Alan Harper had not thought himself capable of

'Just what the hell are you doing? we don't matter anymore is that it? - not me, not the kids, just your damn bloody writing!'

Janet just sat there, still, silent, unresponsive. He knocked the book she'd been reading out of her hand, then and only then did she look up at him. The hate in her eyes and the coldness in her voice took him aback.

'You want food, you make it,' her face twisted into a parody of itself as she walked out of the room.

Clenching his fists until the knuckles showed white, Alan picked up the car keys and walked out of the house.

Alone in the bedroom, Janet sat contemplating her next move. If only Alan would stop his whining then maybe, just maybe, she could come up with a decent idea for a story, but he didn't know when to stop. For years now she'd only done what he wanted, tried to please him as a child tries to be good for Father Christmas, for fear that no presents would be delivered on Christmas night, and yet where were her presents? Where was her reward for being a good wife to

101

Alan? Janet felt suddenly old, and tired, and cheated. Tonight had been the final straw, no longer would he belittle her, no more would she play cook, nanny, housewife to him. An idea began to form in her mind, an idea of a life without Alan's constant whinging, a life without Alan, Alan without a life. A nice little accident could befall him, maybe while he was driving to work, maybe a little food poisoning? She laughed out loud at that, he'd never moan about her cooking again!

'What's so funny mum?' Katrin emerged from the doorway of the bedroom,

'Just something I heard on the radio today love, nothing much'.

Christ, she'd have to be careful, - she didn't want to blow the whole thing before she'd even thought about it seriously

'Go and finish your homework love, I'll get the tea on the go.'

Janet's hands worked mechanically as she prepared the meal, she had no idea where Alan had got to, but she welcomed the fact that he wasn't in, that would be a bit gruesome, contemplating his murder as he sat waiting for his tea. Another giggle escaped her lips, oh, how clever she was, how devious, just like a baddie in one of the books she'd been reading.

Lying alone in bed that night, Janet reached a conclusion where do the most accidents take place? - in the home of course, - simple!

When Alan Harpers car pulled up outside at 11 pm that night, Janet was already asleep, a contented smile playing around her mouth ...

When Alan arrived home the following night he thought he'd come home to the wrong house by mistake. The front room for once was tidy, no hint of a book or even a pen, the smell of cooking filled the air, and Janet herself was there in the kitchen freshly showered, waiting to greet him.

'Something smells good,' he offered, unsure of her mood

'Your all time favourite, made especially for you to say I'm sorry, she smiled up at him, looking young and vulnerable, with her wet hair lying in fronds across her forehead. He hesitated for a second before stepping forward and taking her in his arms, she turned her face up to be kissed, and he responded ardently, sliding his hands inside her bathrobe, caressing the warm flesh he found there.

Her hands worked in his shirt, unbuttoning it with an urgency she'd not shown for a long time, biting his neck and scoring his back with her nails, his need for her becoming obvious, he pushed her away from him with a smile.

'Where are the kids?'

'Stopping overnight with my mother,' she giggled nervously as his hands started to unpeel her robe. 'Patience, lover boy, let me run you a bath first, and if you're a good boy I might come and scrub your back for you.'

With a smile playing on his lips, he let his wife lead him to the bathroom, where he indecently groped her as she bent low over the bath. With a little curtsey and flourish Janet stood back 'your bath sir.' Alan stepped into the steaming water somewhat gingerly, easing himself down slowly, and Janet began to soap him all over, planting little kisses over his neck and body, 'Now lie back, relax and enjoy yourself while I dry my hair.' She smiled the way she always used to smile at him before the children were born, and then flittered out of the room.

Alan's eagerness amused her, could all men be handled so easily with a promise of what was to come? She started to giggle to herself as she plugged her hairdryer into the extension lead.

In the bathroom Alan lay back and relaxed, in the distance he heard the hairdryer begin to drone, he closed his eyes.

Alan was first aware of Janets presence by the cold draught of air that rushed past her through the doorway, she stood looking at him for an intermitable moment, hairdryer held loosely in her hand, 'Ready for dinner yet?'

'I'll be out now love,' he answered with a smile,

Janet moved closer to him, bent down to kiss him, and turned on the hairdryer.

Later, Janet was to remember that last smile of his, the smile that refused to believe what she was about to do, he'd looked up at her as she stood poised above him, and he hadn't understood that she'd really meant to drop in that live, working current.

She'd seen the terror in his eyes, the terror as her fingers had started to unfurl from around the lead, lowering his fate into the bathwater, she'd heard him shout 'no', watched him try to push her away, but she'd already let go, already moved back from his reach.

She'd stood there, watching his body jump and twist, jerking upwards and outwards like some mannequin, a puppet with an invisible puppeteer working the strings, she'd stood there, laughing, until the tears ran down her face, until the strange show ended, until Alan moved no more.

A month after her husbands death (to which the coroner's verdict had ruled misadventure), Janet completed her story.

A smile played around her lips as she typed out the title, 'Accident's will Happen'.

103

The Punishment

by

Karol-An Grogan

She came from a world similar to ours. Her world operated on a different dimension, was more technologically advanced and did not hold with the barbaric practices found here. In her time and space, crimes were dealt with differently. There was no capital punishment in terms of an 'eye for an eye'. To her people it was simple.

The woman was young by our standards, intelligent, gregarious, free floating. Outwardly extrovert, in reality she was far more complex. Like most individuals her inner self hugged secrets that few beheld. Only a privileged handful had been allowed a glimpse into this private sanctuary, the seat of her vulnerability.

Her prison was a cell, eight by eight by eight. No books, television or pictures adorned this room, not one personal artefact to break the monotony. In fact, no visual stimuli at all. Only the absolute bare necessities. A bunk, a chair, a toilet and a machine set into the wall that produced pills which fed her at pre-set times. No comfort eating here, no comfort anything here.

She was invisible to us, surrounded by a force-field as effective as fortress walls and just as impenetrable. Nothing we had could locate or detect her. She was beyond our comprehension.

Crowngate was a new shopping complex, recently completed and opened on the first official day of Spring. Built to blend authentically within the historic setting, it succeeded, almost. Nothing jarred the eye or caused the senses to revolt. In time it would merge beautifully, only its newness rebounded.

The silence was total. Silence so loud it echoed around the empty space and reverberated off the many walls. Silence so profound it hurt. Alone with only her thoughts, her thoughts and her memories, the woman wept.

The conclusive proof of the need for a large precinct is to be found in its use. After the initial onslaught by a curious public, the honeymoon period continued, as if in justification to the enormous outlay. Moderately well off shopkeepers became rich, if not overnight, then relatively soon thereafter, and all involved congratulated each other on the success of the project.

All this was unknown to the woman trapped as she was in her private hell. Each day was the same as the last. Only mealtimes broke the distinction between day and night. Escaping deep inside she would unlock the door and explore slowly, patiently, her precious moments, her cache of truths. Both good and bad she aired them, examined them, took solace, noted regret and resolved not to give up.

The complex was well designed, allowing room for a thoroughfare leading into a roughly rectangular space designed for common usage. A meeting place. Covered and protected it was the ideal spot for relaxation after a busy days shopping. Dotted with cafes and amply supplied with seating, it was a resource that people made the most of. Young and old congregated here. Teenagers crowded around the music stand, girls giggling and jostling, boys flexing and strutting. Tired mothers with whinging toddlers took time to rest, grateful for coffee and cheap ice creams. Elderly folk gathered for a gossip or to play chess. All was active; life revolving in an ever turning circle.

The shock was overwhelming. Her senses attuned to nothingness were obliterated in one powerful stroke. Recoiling instantaneously, her system overloaded, she backed into a corner shivering. Head down, eyes and ears covered she crouched pitifully.

In their wisdom, her people had decided to lower the shield, allowing her visual access to an alien world. A foreign landscape yes, but none-the-less one not so dissimilar to her own that she would not understand.

Regaining control was a slow and painful process. Once retained, and only then, did she open her eyes between parted fingers.

Noise assailed her ears. Music blaring from loudspeakers assaulted her, unfamiliar yet recognisable in form. Overriding this came the sound of voices. Laughter, the same in any language carried through the air, making her smile regardless. To her utter astonishment she found that she understood. The aimless chatter of small children, mindlessly simple, registered. The dialect difficult, but the words meaningful. How could this be? She did not know but the relief was total after her isolation.

Her prison, unseen and unfelt by us, was centrally placed in the square. The shield lifted on all sides afforded her 360 degrees of visibility. She could hear and understand, and she could smell. Faint fragrances of flowers competed with the stronger aroma of ground coffee, making her mouth water, re-awakening memories of past times. Times when she ate and drank normally, laughed and cried, touched and was touched in return. Still this was better, had to be better than what she had before.

Life carried on as normal. People shopped and stopped, made time for conversation and sometimes fun. Spring bulbs were replaced with bedding plants, and the temperature soared in an uncharacteristic English summer. The square heaved with people Mondays through to Saturdays, its popularity growing with every passing week. Only Sundays remained quiet.

She dreaded the Sabbath. For her the square became the dead zone. Her only company, the rustle of debris or the occasional marauding cat. She waited expectantly for the chiming of church bells that signalled togetherness, the meeting of minds and bodies, of humanity, of the end of that long lonely day.

One specific cafe tucked unobtrusively into a secluded corner proved a safe haven from prying eyes, and held special promise for those wishing for obscurity. For no particular reason, apart from its location, it invoked an air of mystery which drew courting couples like magnets. Here secret liaisons took place where whispered words and loving caresses went unnoticed and unremarked. Unnoticed that is, except by one.

The woman felt compelled to watch, regardless of other distractions. Curiosity gave way to habitual surveillance, despite the pain this gave rise to. Compulsive voyeurism became the norm. It triggered for her those deep seated emotions, so tightly held in check. Emotions that promised to tear her apart with their intensity and remembrance. Emotions she could no longer afford to feel.

At first she railed against her incarceration, her spirit demanding action. Screaming and shouting she pounded and tore at her surroundings. Venting anger on her meagre possessions gave some relief, but this was short lived. From rage to tears to sorrow, self pity set in. She became thin, crunching the pills underfoot in her contempt and disgust. Longing overcame her.

With each passing day her despair grew. It became impossible to be part of, but apart from, real life. To experience existence in this way gave no vicarious pleasure. There was no comfort to be had. The punishment, cruel to the extreme, decreed a living death.

Had we known, could we have done anything? As it was we were helpless in our ignorance.

Look Beyond a Tender Smile

by

Tracey Knight

So that's the way it ended... What a waste of a friendship and the unforeseen. He should never have let his heart rule his head but rational thought never raises an eyebrow when you've fallen in love. Things which seem possible become impossible and a handsome look or wayward smile often holds something cold and vile. Life becomes one big illusion, nothing stays constant for very long especially the truth.

Well the truth creates its own shape and form which it changes to suit the appropriate occasion. Then there comes the line between fantasy and reality which merges into one. Even in your sleeping hours your mind does not stop to rest, it never tires and it longs to explore to create a master piece which everyone will remember.

When you have connected with another person you both begin to recognize things which you had never noticed before and inside a vast amount of creative energy is just ready to burst forth. They say there is nothing more soul destroying than recounting the past and trying to fathom out what you did wrong and when the past holds so much more than the present then it is very easy to drift back within those memories.

The room was on the top floor, it faced south towards the railway embankment and the new housing estates beyond. It was mid September and already the nights were drawing in and the leaves were falling from the trees to hide the grey pavements down below. In the room however the air was warm and still, the atmosphere was mixed, one minute it was calm and the next minute it was loud and chaotic. The room was full of people with faces which had grown accustomed to listening, paying attention and looking thoughtful even if they didn't understand what was going on or if they even cared. Today no one felt like learning, some heads turned towards the noises and sights that beckoned outside the glass wall. Others sat talking, more interested in the latest gossip and about last night's outing to the local disco than what was happening there and then.

At the front sat in a huddle were a select few who either had poor eyesight or they had genuinely came to learn. It was these few who were the ones who were going to pass, the others didn't have a chance and it wasn't because they were less able it was because they didn't care, they just didn't have any faith in their own abilities.

On the end of the front row sat a shy and retiring thing but how wrong first impressions can be. Helen was a little different from the rest, she was slightly older and definitely more mature than anybody else in that room, on that day in question. During that afternoon in all the fuss and confusion a deeper misunderstanding began. Like a baby in the womb something had begun to grow and like the baby it could only be stopped by a drastic measure.

It wasn't an intentional thing, it was never meant to happen but it did. It began when everything was decaying and dying, it didn't seem to have any clearly defined beginning although the end was brightly highlighted. Perhaps it started when they first met but that is far too much of a cliche but they do say that it takes less than ten seconds to fall in love with someone and the rest of your life trying to figure out what you saw in them.

Imagine a situation in which there are boundaries and both parties understand the rules but sometimes rules are just there to be broken and in this case they were.

A man stood leaning against a table, his eyes averted to something moving out of the corner of his eye, that something he found most appealing. His stare traced the outline of this new figure and then without flinching he looked over her head to the row behind. He ran his fingers through his hair, stretched and yawned, then he smiled. Was he tired or was the smile a reminder of something pleasant?

He was good looking, fresh faced and intriguing but it wasn't that which made him likeable. It was his character, his boyish charm and rebellious attitude which made him stand out above everyone else and that is what she noticed.

Helen was a late enrolee and had only started the course a week ago but already she had decided that this teacher was different. He was funny, witty and receptive. He made the subject interesting and what is more he gave her the incentive to get up on those cold dark mornings, when really she would have rather have overslept and stayed in that warm, snug environment of her bed.

They hit it off straight away chatting about this and that but nothing in particular, just small talk but he was always so enthusiastic and she was always spellbound as if the words that came from his lips were magical. Slowly they began to build up a rapport, they were always on the same wavelength as if they had learned the secret art of telepathy, he always knew that when no one else would know the answer she always would. They were like a comedy duet, one telling the story and the other giving the punch-line. He overflowed with confidence, he was so bubbly, but in all probability he was putting on an act and to cover up his weaknesses which were plentiful. If their relationship had remained like this then things would have turned out for the better but as life is a lesson and sometimes we have to learn the hard way, which is only natural, they too crossed the line between right and wrong and learned the lesson the hard way.

Helen woke up to find thick snow on the ground, it was the first of the year. Everything was quiet and still outside and as usual the bus didn't make it up the steep bank, so instead she had to rush half a mile through the town to the train station.

When she eventually arrived in the city, she was already an hour late so she didn't bother rushing, she made her way through the old market place looking at the shop displays as she walked past. As she crossed the road to Albert Street a sudden gust of wind took her scarf and whilst turning round to catch it, she didn't look to see where she was going and bang, she bumped into something very solid coming the other way which unbalanced her and she ended up sitting smack down on the cold, wet pavement. Feeling like a helium balloon about to explode she looked up and then began to blush. That immovable object was Nick, they both looked at each other and then Nick helped her up.

Nick spoke first: 'Are you alright?'

'Yes, I'm fine, except now I'm a little wet.' She smiled and then shivered.

Nick looked sympathetic and asked Helen if she didn't have a lesson would she like to have a drink with him. Helen was quite astonished at this invitation but she was intrigued to find out more about this wild card so she agreed.

They walked side by side along the slushy pavements sometimes brushing each others arms as they moved to avoid other pedestrians coming towards them.

Eventually they stopped at a car park which ran alongside the canal. His car was a large red capri, normally she would have thought twice about getting in a car with a stranger but she felt safe with Nick. They drove through the busy city traffic and stopped some miles out at a small family run pub.

When they walked in all eyes turned towards them, the patrons looked like farmers or game keepers in their green jackets and tweed caps. One man was sat near the open hearth smoking a pipe and another was reading a newspaper. Then there were some younger men propping up the bar and telling dirty jokes. Nick went up to them and started chatting whilst Helen stood there feeling out of place, so she went and sat next to one of the sash windows and started fiddling with the cardboard beer mats. She suddenly felt awkward and wondered what the hell she was doing here with this man, her superior. Did he like her and if he did, what was going to happen next?

In a short space of time that question was answered. He came back with two packets of cheese and onion crisps and two pints of cider, he took the chair directly opposite her. Helen began to feel self conscious, she could not look him straight in the eye because he had such an intense stare, it made her feel threatened and also she was worried that if he looked too deeply he might discover the truth hidden behind her eyes.

He put down his drink and started rubbing his left eye, then he spoke.

'It was funny bumping into you like that, I was thinking about you at the time as well.'

Helen felt her stomach knot and her throat went suddenly dry and tight.

'Oh I hope you were thinking only kindly thoughts of me?' She smiled but Nick seemed very stern and then he replied.

'It's my birthday next week and I was wondering if you would like to come along, you can bring a friend if you want.' For the first time he looked at the floor.

Helen could not believe what she had just heard and she didn't need any encouragement or time to come to a decision.

'Ah, yes I would like to come, what day is it though?'

'It's next Wednesday, is that alright?'

'Oh yes that's fine.'

Then there was a silence. Helen already knew it was his Birthday but she could never have guessed that he would invite her to it. He was twenty-five going on twenty-six but he looked so much younger. He had shoulder length brown hair and green eyes. She couldn't put her finger on what it was that had made her feel that this man was special. Could it be his smile which lit up his face and showed up his two dimples and crooked teeth or could it be his weird sense of humour. Who knows, but one thing is for sure he made her feel so special and wanted and at that moment she didn't have any cares in the world.

They had another drink and then left to travel back to the city, after they had spent two and a half hours of getting to know each other.

110

When they parked back at the canal car park, Nick leaned over and put his arms tightly around Helen's shoulders and as she went to leave he pecked her gently upon her cheek.

She felt so happy and she felt she could face anyone but she knew it wasn't right to deceive her family, friends and the college but deceive them she did and nobody caught on.

Then came the day she had been waiting for, Nick's birthday. She had told her parents that she was staying at a friend's house the night and that she would be back the following evening. They were fine and when five o'clock in the afternoon came she breathed a huge sigh of relief.

She met him at the car park. It was too risky waiting for him outside college. She wished him a Happy Birthday and gave him his card. He leaned forward and kissed her and then lifted her off the ground and swung her round, she indeed felt like she was walking on upon air.

It was almost an hour's drive to his house and when they stopped it was dusk. he house was a two bedroomed mid terrace house in a run down cul-de-sac. She had reservations but by now it was too late to back down. He was also nervous wandering if he was doing the right thing.

The party went smoothly and she seemed to mix well with his friends even though they were several years older than her and they all had degrees in various disciplines. Some of them were a little dubious however and warned her that it couldn't last and that they were both playing with fire and one of them was sure to get burned, but she wasn't listening to them.

That night she slept in his bed, whilst he slept on the floor as some of his friends had stayed over. Several times she awoke to hear him snoring and could make out the outline of his body in the moonlight. It was him however who awoke first in the morning and went downstairs to think. He hadn't the heart to wake her up as, she looked so peaceful and serene.

It was a real frosty morning but the sun was out and the birds were in full chorus outside in the overgrown apple tree. What should he do was the question he was asking himself. The truth was obvious but painful, he knew this time however his feelings would have to be put aside.

He liked Helen a lot but he wasn't good enough for her. He had only just finished a long standing relationship with another girl and he could not let Helen be the rebound. It wasn't fair for her and besides she was too young to be stuck with him. She had many more years yet to decide what she wanted to do and if she had decided, then it would have been a waste of up and coming talent.

So on the way back he let her down gently if that is possible. She didn't say anything but she didn't have to, it was all written upon her face.

Her anger and bitterness for what she saw as rejection led her to tell a friend and that friend decided to tell someone else and so on. Until some weeks later Nick was called into the Head's office and without any written warning, he was sacked on the spot.

Helen still cared about him and hated herself even more when she found out what had happened but it was out of her hands.

So the end of term came and he disappeared, vanished into thin air. She knew she would never see him again and she tried to look forward to the long hot summer days ahead and if that wasn't enough, in a year or so she would be putting all of her energies into passing a degree.

She would never forget him, for it isn't often that you meet someone who you've felt you have known all your life and that if things were different perhaps you would have shared the rest of your life with. The love they had shared was innocent, but necessity didn't understand that, it pulled them apart to do different things and to be somebody else's love.

Political Upheaval

by

Mark A Arnold

Raindrops race each other down the windowpanes in my room. The rain beats the glass like pearl barley against a drum; tap, patter, patter, hummm... tap, tap... tap, tap, tap... the ticker tape spews out of the machine in the telegraphic's room, falling like spaghetti into the wicker basket below the desk. Endless coded papers from them to me, me to him and back again.

It's an Indian summer back in Britain, I'm told; humid and hot, yet it isn't muggy here in India; ironic really, Delhi is scorched dry, the earth is cracked by the relentless heat of a bare sun. The machine still taps out it's paper gossip... tap, tap, hum; tap, tap...

A mosquito lands gently on my arm and suffers a quick death before biting; the damn things are everywhere, the heat hasn't deterred them yet. Too many bodies up for grabs, hot, sweating, boiling. Too hot for an Englishman; too far from the lush greenery of home; too damn bad I'm stuck here.

Tap, tap, hum; tap, tap... *'Priority message'*... *'Attention P T Johnson, British Consulate, New Delhi.. Meet Houseman, 17.30 today to arrange a shooting party for the Consul... End... Class 5... RCT London.'*

Now, this is unusual. A class 5 message through class 2 channels. Some sort of mistake, I assume, at London end. Best sort it out with the Consulate. No wonder nothing secret stays that way for long around here.

Funny though; most social arrangements come through here, class 2; this message is class 5, not my department at all. Tap, tap, hum, tap, tap...

Ring the consulate. Ouch! These black Bakelite phones get so hot in the sunlight. Damn. No answer, try again. Tap, tap, tap.

'Yes, can I have the Department of Information, please?... Yes, I'll wait. My name?... of course... it's Corby; J B from Telegraphics (Incoming).'

'Yes, Hello. I'm afraid I seem to have received a message that is above my class authorization, sir. I assume I pass it on to you? I do; right, it's... Oh, I am sorry Mr Johnson, yes I do understand, not over the phone. Class 5 sir. Who is it from? The initials are RCT, a London based message...

'... Hello, Hello? Sir, are you still there? 'At once? Bring it to you personally, yes sir. Thank you.

'... that's correct, J B Corby, Telegraphics (Incoming), based at the Patna Market Street office. Certainly, right away sir... Rear of the Consulate, yes sir. Thank you.'

Well, this is a turn up for the books. I'm to meet a class 5 representative; not an everyday occurrence, in fact not an any day occurrence, if the truth be known. Johnson, Houseman, RCT London, Class 5, very strange. It's all beyond me.

Grief! I thought it was hot in the office but it's like a furnace in these narrow streets. The sun reflects off the buildings, hitting me from all sides. Heat floats on the air and mixes with the spicy aromas that creep from the shop fronts. It's becoming hard to breathe. At last, here it is, the Consulate building. Hello? This is a bit cloak and dagger. Gloves, guns and wide-brimmed hats?

'Hello. Which of you gentlemen is the class 5 represen... ummph!... What the hell are you doing?'

Christ! A syringe? What for? They can't do this... should deliver the message... feel dizzy, so very dizzy... going to be sick... going to...

The grey blanket fades from before my eyes and a small room; a printing room, I guess, from the machinery; swims slowly into focus. The ineffectual little man before me, smiles kindly and drops the hammer head deftly onto the index finger of my right hand. White hot pain tears the scream from my lungs, a long rasping sigh.

...fifty-five, fifty-six, fifty-seven... the pain thumps in my finger, counting the seconds and through inches of tears, I see the hammer lift, feel it fall again and my left hand ignites. The pain; a scream, loud this time; consciousness slips away.

Again, I open my eyes to the room, pain in each hand, thumping; the same weasely little man smiles. Small man smiling. How did I intercept the message? I didn't intercept it. It just came through telegraphics. yes, of course, the printer. It can't be impossible, it happened! I'm not lying. No I'm not! Oh please, not again.

I feel my finger splinter and the chill heat is twice as freezing-hot as before. I'm going to faint, thank God! A needle bites my arm; 'a cocktail', he says, 'amphetamines: speed, purple-hearts, to keep me awake, so I'll enjoy the show.' The cocktail is cold in my arm; fainting, dreamlike... but no, I'm not being allowed to faint, my heartbeat drums a tattoo in my ears; every detail of the room is heightened including the pain which screams along my arms from my fingers.

114

If I tell him how I got hold of the message and who I work for, he promises to stop tapping the stiff-bristled brush against the place where my nails used to be. Who do I work for? No, not the Foreign Office; who do I really work for?

What do you want me to say, smiling elfin man? Germans? Russians? Indian Nationalists? I'll say anything, anything as long as you take the brush away, please? please?

The hammer lifts. Little smiling man.

I realise I should not have had class 5 information. It just came. No, not impossible, true! I have no more answers.

My silence brings the hammer down again. I dearly want to faint, but the needle has already ensured my consciousness. Cut my arms off! Stop the pain! I have no other answers. Hammer and hairbrush take turns; both, ask me for a confession of the unknown... fifty-five, fifty-six, fifty-seven... the pain in my fingers counts the seconds... counts the brushes' bites... tap, tap, tap... tap, tap, tap... the pain can get no worse.

They put little bits of paper in my mouth, fifteen or so.

'... Red dragons... myriad Chinese dreams... LSD. Phencyclidine; to forget... a dream forever... '

Tap, tap, tap... the rain runs down the window... tap, tap, tap...

'Yes doctor, this one is Mr Corby: J B Corby. He's been with us, ohhh, about thirteen years now. Not much to say for himself; have you Mr Corby? Never speaks. Introversion, extreme. He was caught up in the political upheaval in India in 1955; had a nervous breakdown; put his hands into a printing machine, as far as they could gather. Discharged from the Foreign Office about the time that P T Johnson took over as the Consul in New Delhi. There was that psychopath, Horseman or was it Houseman? The one that shot the Consul and some of the staff. Terrible uproar in the papers at the time. A little before your time, I guess... Mr Corby causes us very little trouble really; although he doesn't like one of the B-wing doctors; small, happy fellow, you've probably already met him. Such a violent reaction from Mr Corby that we had to transfer him over here. We also have to keep him away from Mr Evans, Room 6; you've already seen him... that's right; 'The Grinning Elf'. Can't understand why, but, there you go.

'Anyway, Mr Corby just stares out of the window; but he will keep tapping his thumbs on the table, never stops. Irritating after a while.'

...tap, tap; tap, tap; tap, tap...

'Typewriter Corby' they call him.

'Now then Doctor. Your next charge is Mr Allen, Room 13... '

...Tap, tap; tap, tap; tap, tap...

...Tap, tap; tap, tap; tap, tap...

The tape spews out of the machine... Tap, tap; tap, tap... falling like spaghetti into the wicker basket below... Tap, tap; tap, tap; tap, tap...

Marguerite

by

Judy Dinnen

This story is dedicated to Helen Bridgewater, who died of cancer, April 1992.

M T sighed and slowly and carefully replaced her cup in the saucer. She listened, suddenly aware of silence, broken only by a distant dog bark. She sat still on the cane chair, aware not only of intermittent sounds, but also of the sounds of the past. She relived those last few days of doors banging, voices shouting, music beating loudly and glasses clinking. And now Mick had gone, - gone on the road to adulthood, the beginning of a University degree course; a new world, that would belong to Mick, that would be fashioned and developed by him and countless other human beings, whose faces she did not know, in buildings she had only briefly visited, whose sounds she had not had time to listen to.

She was left in a new space, a new quietness, that belonged to her alone. She knew she needed to explore it and fill it with new sounds; sounds that belonged to her, that sang of her presence, that responded to her new needs, as a woman, not as a mother, but as a woman of forty-five with a future to fill. She acknowledged the challenge and knew that soon she would rise to meet it, but for the moment she just sat. She allowed the world and its noises to swarm around her as they wished and she made no attempt to sort or reject them.

She idly pressed the button on the radio and Beethoven's last symphony flooded the room. The familiar melody wafted through M T's head, but her mind was like a sea shore, washed afresh by wave after wave; each one bringing with it new thoughts, new images and new memories that then retreated.

She saw the huge, grey University block where she had left Mick, just two hours ago. It did not please her architecturally, being somewhat forbidding in its size and lacking any interesting characteristics, but that did not deter Mick. He was already talking to a fellow student, his dark eyes lapping over the boy's face taking in every detail, then darting to the entrance door to see how far they had to carry their cases. She stood on the greensward, giving a final wave, as the two figures receded towards the unprepossessing building, that was to be their new world; Mick's tall, dark figure and the shorter, stockier one beside him.

MT Felt pleased for him, but sad that Michael was not there to share it with them. Her lip trembled as she thought of Michael. She saw his face, pale and thoughtful, as he lay in bed, day after day, for nearly two months. She thought tenderly of his courageous smile, his nagging worries about leaving her and Mick. She smiled as she felt a wave of warmth envelope her, the warmth that intensified over those last months, a warmth that only they shared. She felt they had a private bond, perhaps a new place or even a new dimension, where they had been together. That was her secret comfort, that she could draw around herself at moments like these. Tears pricked her eyes and yet she smiled, thankful for the warmth of their love.

The choral symphony was underway, but MT switched it off abruptly; the sounds raced ahead too quickly, not suited to the meandering, healing pace of her thoughts. The silence seemed all the more intense and she wondered if she would get used to it or even come to enjoy it maybe. Her life had been so full of noise, as Mick's friends listened to rave music or raided the fridge, noise that had not seemed to bother Michael as he lay upstairs. He seemed to need some sense of life continuing and enjoyed the obvious pleasure that Mick derived from his many friends.

Then Michael had died. MT sat very still in the darkening room as her mind ran through the events of that night - that moment she had dreaded, but yet which brought such sweet relief to Michael, as he gave up the unequal struggle for life. He was fifty-two and life had seemed so full of promise. They had talked about going abroad; there had been a possibility of a post in Nigeria. They had pored over maps, discussed it with friends, worried about Mick's schooling and his final exams. Then there were routine medical checks when the tumour had been found. Nigeria was instantly forgotten and the world of heat, mosquito nets, visas, new sights and sounds of the tropics gave way to one of the hospital, curtained beds, doctors, explanations, the operation and all its concomitant fears and hopes. That all seemed so long ago, though in fact it was only just over six months, six extraordinary months, when their cosy, familiar world had changed shape and not as they had planned.

MT had already given in her notice at the surgery, just as well really, as it had allowed her time to be with Michael; to spend as much time as she could at his bedside. Even when he was sleeping she liked to sit there and muse, to reminisce on their life together, just as she was now. She felt she was thus able to tie together her ideas, to give time to the varied emotions that came flooding in and even write about them in her notebook. In fact her note book had become her constant companion; it was almost a diary really. She confided in it, what was happening each day and turn her harshest feelings into wild winds, or furious waves - she loved the sea. One day she showed her writing to Michael. He was feeling fairly well, shortly after coming home again. He asked her something about the time - did she find it dragging or wouldn't she like to go away for a few days?

'No!' She gasped emphatically; for she could not bear the thought of going further afield than the local supermarket. So she gingerly showed him a page in her book, written just after his operation. She was concerned lest he might not be able to cope with her feelings, which were fairly vividly expressed. Tears sprang into his eyes as they journeyed across the scrawled words, which were full of love as well as pain. He reached out for her hand and squeezed it with great tenderness.

'I'm glad you've got such a valuable companion,' he said, somewhat ambiguously.

MT glanced at the small blue book, with its watery pattern. It lay on the table with her pen beside it; the pen Michael had given her for Christmas. It was a special gift, for it seemed that Michael was endorsing her writing, almost that he was part of it, which indeed he was. Not many pages would pass without some reference to Michael, and in a way it allowed him to continue living, after May the fourth 1985, the day he squeezed her hand for the last time and closed his eyes to the world. He lived on in her words and she found that after he had gone, in the literal sense, that she did not only write of the cancer and the pain of loss and separation, she wrote also about Michael as he had been, of things they had done together, friends and holidays they had shared, concerts they had been to, and of course Mick their only son and the slight regret at not having had any more children. She filled pages with endless descriptions bound up in happiness, but tinged with sorrow.

MT had been invited to see a counsellor at the hospice and she did go once or twice. She had shown the woman her notebook and the counsellor had found it very moving. She had even asked if she might reproduce a page or two in the hospice newsletter, as she felt it might well be of help to other relatives, in similar circumstances. MT readily agreed, though she went home and re-read possible pages with a fresh eye, wondering how it would sound to other people and whether anyone else could possibly feel quite how she felt. Maybe her words might enter the space of some other poor soul going through this vacuum, this unreal world, which one feels nobody else has ever experienced.

MT lifted the small blue notebook. She opened it and began to write - 'Friday 30th Sept. 1985. I took Mick to University. A new world is opening up for him, though of course, with him, he still brings cases from home. Inside him folded like a precious flower are the embryos of ideas, feelings and understanding yet to open and grow.

'I must now pick up my bags and begin my own new journey. Maybe I need to buy a timetable and a map, so that I can plan where I am going.'

The Lodger

by

Lynne Hackles

On the thirtieth of January the lodger - tall, white haired and bone jutting gaunt - ascended the stairs for the first time. And disappeared into the room at the top of the house.

By mid-February the ladies were beginning to worry.

'You've never heard him Mum? Never?' Asked Sarah.

Mrs Parsons, marble white, lay on the bed like a knight's lady carved on a tomb lid. Through all her stillness the old lady's mind raged and her eyelids moved.

Two blinks. No.

Could it be true? Had Mr Hammond been ensconced in the attic for two whole weeks? Impossible.

'I've not seen him since he moved in but, surely while I was out at work he must have come downstairs? Gone to the shops?'

Two blinks. No.

Perhaps he had died or left without saying. No. He had paid three months rent in advance. He would not have gone away. Death then was the answer.

Death was always the answer, thought Sarah. She stood, the administering angel at the coffin foot of her mother's bed. Escape could only come through death. Her own or her mother's. Two lonely women. One imprisoned in paralysed flesh. The other blood tied to her.

The lodger was supposed to have eased their financial burden. His rent money supplemented the income from Sarah's part-time job. But she had hoped for more than money. Nightly she had prayed for a friend, someone to help her cope with the rotting body and eternally beating heart of the thing she called Mother.

Anger rose volcanically inside her. Now she had another rotting body to contend with. She burned at the thought. Her temper - like lava - overspilled. Blistering, bubbling, it flowed through the old house. Up and up the stairs it seethed, dragging Sarah to the attics.

And then, on the topmost stair - subsidence. Temper, knees, shoulders, spirit. The poor man could not help dying.

121

Sarah crept to his door. A floorboard creaked. Her hand gripped the door-knob. The wind moaned in the rafters. A golden thread of light squeezed out of the keyhole. She put her ear against the door panel and listened. From the room came the sounds of children laughing, a chair rocking, hot coals sputtering.

From the room came the smell of toasting muffins, brewing tea, floating chalk dust.

She held her breath. Turned the knob. Opened the door.

Mr Hammond, in the deep armchair, by the silent radio, looked up and smiled.

'Welcome,' he said. His eyes were bright and his sunken cheeks flushed pink. 'Sit down.'

Sarah sat in the other armchair on the opposite side of the empty fireplace.

'I'm sorry to disturb you Mr Hammond, but mother and I had not seen you and we were rather worried.'

The old gentleman nodded. 'I told you I would be no trouble. Make no noise. That you would not know I was here.'

Now Sarah nodded. 'Of course', - and rose to leave. There was nothing else to say. He was not dead. He looked well. At the door she turned. 'I was wondering, Mr Hammond, if... ' She paused. 'if you would mind talking to mother sometimes. I have to work mornings and she gets lonely.'

'I should be delighted, Miss Parsons. Delighted.'

A crackling cold waited on the landing. Frosty ferns were sketched on the skylight. Sarah pulled her cardigan closer and shivered. It had been so warm in the room. So warm and yet... There was no fire.

Mrs Parsons had company the next morning. More than she had ever ex-pected.

Sarah, sitting at her desk in the office, sipped coffee alone - surrounded by young girls with spiky hair and long red nails, gossiping about boyfriends. No-one had time for a middle aged spinster.

Later, at home, she warmed soup for lunch. As she spoon fed the old lady she noticed how bright her eyes were, how flushed her cheeks.

'Mum, what's happened?' And then she guessed. 'Has Mr Hammond been to see you?'

One blink and an added twinkle to the eye.

Fancy Mr Hammond producing such an effect.

That evening Sarah climbed to the attic but she did not see the lodger. With the ice painted skylight above her and the threadbare carpet beneath she sat on the top stair listening to the music, the voices, the singing and laughter - creep-

122

ing through the keyhole, seeping through the panelling, oozing beneath the door. For long hours she sat soaking up the warmth from the empty fireplace on the lodger's side of the attic door.

In the frozen midnight she made her way to bed and lay, confused between snowy sheets.

Mr Hammond visited Mrs Parsons the next day. And the next and the next. He had time for her. Centuries of time.

Sarah returned from the office each day to see new life in her mother's face. Sarah sat on the topmost stair each night to listen at the lodger's door.

One Wednesday in early March, she had a bad headache and was sent home mid morning. Home unexpectedly.

Pain scratched at her eyes as she stood on the step, fumbling in her bag for the house key. Pain throbbed in time to the music, pulsated to the loud chatter. A golden thread of light squeezed out of the keyhole. Light, warmth, music, voices. She knew all would vanish at her entrance.

She stepped back and her boots crunched the stiff white grass. The house windows burned sunshine rectangles on the chilly garden. An intruder, she peeped through the glass, through the lace net curtains and deeper into the room.

Eyes widened, mouth opened, knees buckled, fingers gripped the sill.

Her mother. Her mother in tiers of lilac silk, was dancing with Mr Hammond. Porcelain elegant, the figures whirled in and out between the other couples. Fairy light and agile as youth they waltzed in the brightness. And in the ice-held garden Sarah's mind screamed. Mother can't move. She can't move.

Shaking hands held the key, opened the door to the quiet dimness of a vast empty house. Empty save for the white statue on the bed, the lodger in the chair.

Sarah walked into the silence. 'I'm not well,' she moaned and slid to the floor.

Mr Hammond's skeletal hands patted her face, held a brandy glass to her lips. 'Miss Parsons, are you all right? Should I call for a doctor?'

He was all concern. With a mysterious strength he lifted her to a chair. 'You work too hard. The office. Your mother. You should think of yourself sometimes. Get away from it all.'

Slumped in the chair she searched his eyes and found, in their cavernous depths - a lilac dress, a child in velvet breeches, horses, candlelight, carriages.

Her pain slipped away and a tingling glowing warmth crept in to replace it.

That night she climbed the stairs to thank him for his kindness. Outside his door she hesitated - listened for the joyous sounds, reached out to experience the warmth.

There was nothing.

She knocked and entered to his command.

In the attic, years of shadows jostled with icy beams of moonlight.

'I have been waiting for you,' said Mr Hammond.

He stood to join the shadows. Stars sparkled in his hair. The moon shone from the caves of his eyes. he reached out a hand to touch her and his bones glittered like ropes of diamonds beneath the cobweb skin. He tugged at her innermost thoughts - the mighty life draining struggle between the love for her mother and her own need to escape. Her pain and loneliness gave him substance. She blinked and looked up at the lodger - tall, white-haired and bone jutting gaunt.

'Who are you?' Sarah asked.

'Help,' he replied.

'Help for me? For mother?'

He nodded.

'Where have you come from?'

'Time,' he replied.

He waved a hand to illuminate the attic. Children rolled from the vanishing shadows. A burning log spluttered in the hearth. A nurse picked up toys and rubbed the blackboard clean. 'The nursery,' explained Mr Hammond.

He led her down the stairs and into the music filled living room.

Mrs Parsons was playing the piano. A gentleman in dove grey suit, whiskers twitching, waited to turn the music sheet. Her mother saw her and smiled.

Mr Hammond guided Sarah along the passage.

'A walk outside, Miss Parsons?' He held open the door.

Sunshine, rose scent, bruised grass, splashing water, chirruping birds waited.

'Escape,' whispered Mr Hammond.

Sarah ventured forth, lifting the long turquoise gown from the pathway. Dropping the years with each step.

A young man hurried across the lawn to join her.

The lodger smiled and closed the door.

124

Private Tutorial

by

Katherine Roberts

John Stanton, BSc, PhD, watched his brand new class snatch up their books and bounce, chattering gaily, from the lecture theatre. All so young and innocent, each one bubbling with girlish charm. His eyes followed their swinging hips, their long, tanned legs disappearing tantalisingly under skirts even shorter than last year. Oh, how he loved Freshers!

His gaze lingered on one blond girl who seemed quiet and removed from the crowd. Her big blue eyes peeped shyly at him from beneath her fringe, perhaps sensing his scrutiny. John felt his blood stir.

The girl's name was Anna, and she had accepted his offer to go over her essay in his room tonight. They nearly always fell for that one - John never ceased to be amazed at how naive Freshers could be. Surely he had never been so gullible, all those years ago?

He looked at the clock. It had been a present from a girl back in the days when he used to have normal relationships. He did not really know why he kept it. All that wining and dining, the cajoling and creeping, and putting up with her excuses. She had been like all the rest - a selfish bitch. Well, he was through with all that. From now on, John Stanton would have his women where and when he wanted them.

Eight o'clock. John took some books down from the shelf. He had to make a show of sincerity. There was no sense in scaring the girl away immediately.

Eight fifteen. He fixed himself a drink and checked his supplies. Hundreds of bottles nestled in the specially converted cabinet, cheap spirits and liqueurs jostling for space with a vast collection of tonic waters and soft drinks in their own little bottles. My faithful babies, he thought, lifting one of the water bottles to the light. No-one could possibly guess what it really contained.

Eight thirty. He closed the drinks cabinet and emptied his glass. She was late. An anxious thought crossed his mind that some idiot had warned her off. There were one or two students who had complained of his advances, but they were in the minority. Those who succumbed usually remembered little of their night of enlightenment. They might have their suspicions, but so far nothing concrete had been proved against him.

125

A soft tap on the door made him smile. He admitted Anna, forcing himself to look at her face instead of her lovely legs. There would be plenty of time for that later.

'Put those on the table, and let me take your coat,' he instructed, surprised at the amount of work she had brought with her. Files and books spilled out of her arms to join his own volumes. She must take her studies too seriously, he thought, as he peeled the coat from her thin shoulders.

'It's good of you to give me personal tuition like this, Dr Stanton,' Anna said. 'I am really stuck with that last essay you gave us.' She sat at the table and pulled out a pair of spectacles. 'What exactly did you mean by family feuds?'

John pulled up a chair beside her with an inward sigh. Far too serious for such a pretty girl, he decided as she questioned him non-stop on the meaning of his lectures. She looked to be a hard worker - not terribly clever, but dedicated. She probably did not have time for much of a social life. In which case he would be doing her a favour later on tonight.

'Dr Stanton?' John snapped back to the present with a start, to find Anna frowning at him. 'Am I tiring you?' she asked.

'Not at all, my dear Anna. However, I think that is enough work for tonight. I cannot write the essay for you. You must go away and think about the ideas we have discussed, and don't worry too much. First year course work counts very little towards your degree.'

She was staring at him with those wide blue eyes, having removed her glasses at last. It was all John could do to keep his tone casual.

'How about a drink before you go?' he asked.

'Thank you very much, Dr Stanton. But I think I'd better make a start on this essay.'

John moved across to the drinks cabinet, carefully neutral. 'Well, I'm having one anyway. Are you sure you won't join me?' Anna hesitated, looking at her watch. 'We can talk about the relevance of your course-work.'

'All right. But just a mineral water, please.'

Got her!

John picked one of his special bottles out for her, opened it, and placed it on a low table by the sofa along with an ornate glass. He waved Anna over.

'Might as well make yourself comfortable.' He groped in a cupboard and found some salted nuts, which he added to the low table. 'Help yourself. I'm just going to the bathroom.'

He lingered in the toilet before returning to the room and selecting a CD. 'I hope you like Vangelis?' He glanced across to where Anna was daintily sipping her drink.

'Sure,' she murmured, blinking as the music surged around her.

John dimmed the lights before joining her on the sofa, trying to assess if the 'water' was taking effect. 'Now, about that course-work...' he began.

Anna frowned, taking another gulp. 'The course-work,' she repeated.

'Yes. I was saying earlier that your first year essays do not count much towards your final marks. When you get to your second year, things begin to be more serious.' She was only half listening to him, letting her gaze roam around the room.

'But you need not worry, Anna.' John took hold of her hand and gently began to stroke it. 'I'll always be here when you need me.'

She had not withdrawn her hand, which was a good sign. John felt the excitement building inside him. He leaned across to take some nuts, then fed them to her one by one.

'Do you like cashews?' he asked as she licked the salt from his fingers.

'Is what that they are?' she mumbled, and he smiled.

'They make me thirsty,' she admitted, draining her glass.

John jumped to his feet. 'Forgive me, my dear Anna! I'll get you another.'

The second bottle disappeared quicker than the first, by which time the girl was lolling over the arm of his sofa, totally relaxed. He allowed himself the luxury of unbuttoning her blouse, slowly, watching all the time for an adverse reaction. He did not really expect resistance at this stage, and Anna offered none.

She giggled as he squeezed her breasts. Suddenly he could contain himself no longer. Pushing up her skirt, he pinned her against the sofa. The zipper on his trousers stuck, and he cursed it fluently. His desire was becoming more painful by the second, accentuated by the girl's squirming underneath him.

'Dr... con... dom?' she slurred as he finally freed himself. She must be joking if she thought he was going to use one of those! Anna struggled briefly before the music engulfed him in a moment of pure ecstasy.

John was whistling as he entered the staff common room the following morning. He had left Anna sleeping it off with a note to make herself some coffee before she returned to her lodgings.

'You're happy today, John,' remarked one of his fellow lecturers. 'Must have scored last night?'

'Certainly did! Wow, what a night!' A ripple of laughter ran around the room - most of the staff were fully aware of his reputation.

'Seriously though, John, you'd best keep away from that blond. Such a pretty little thing, you'd never guess by looking at her that she's got Aids. Poor lass, it's such a shame. Works so hard, too.' Everyone else murmured their sympathy, but John's blood turned to ice. He felt as if someone had just dropped an enormous boulder into his stomach.

'What's her name?' he whispered through dry lips, already fearing the answer.

'Are you all right, John?' The room had gone quiet. Everyone was staring at him.

'Her name, I said! What's her name?' He seized the informant by his collar and shook him violently.

'Steady on, John! I'll tell you if you'll just stop strangling me. She's called Miss Smythe - I think her first name's Anna.'

What's in a Name

by

Lorne Richardson

It is funny how life settles down and changes its pattern. Take names for instance.

Not long after I had met Nora and decided that this was the girl I wanted to marry, her name sounded to me like that of a lovely star in a musical comedy.

I had met or heard of other Nora's, of course, but this one was different to me.

That was eight years ago. I don't know if there is any truth in it; and men are just as bad; but once they have got their man some women seem to let themselves go.

Nora had been quite a flier at the end of school and afterwards, I heard. Not promiscuous sexually apparently, though she had the looks and vivacity to awaken any male's ardour, and dressed to kill.

Now, I was compelled to admit from that point of view that she was nothing out of the ordinary any more than her name was, and had, in fact, put on rather too much weight.

I was wishing she was called Felicity or Daphne or Stephenie and lived up to it. I knew that I had become disenchanted and sometimes showed it I am afraid,

'Nora,' I shouted one morning, flinching at the harsh sound of it escaping from my lips and not for the first time. 'Where is the pen I always keep by the telephone?'

I was in a bad temper as I had stepped on the ballpoint that is my constant companion. I depend a lot on notes and hurry to jot things down that come into my head before they fly out again in less than a minute.

Living together with anyone, of course, reveals different habits sometimes irritating. Nora is one of those people who cause pens to disappear and grab any other in sight rather than look for the first one; while I keep them where I want them. Then suddenly, like now, I can't find any.

Getting off to the office needs routine timing, and I was running late already by the time Nora produced the telephone pen from a handbag.

You couldn't call her cowed: 'Hurry up, Jack,' she said, 'you are going to be late and there are plenty of pens in the office.'

I was late, of course, and resentful, but it probably wasn't noticed.

I suppose I am romantic or sentimental or both. I've always been like that, and marrying a lovely girl was real fulfilment at the time, so I had grown bitter.

More husbands seem to use their wives for peace and comfort than delight in showing them off, revelling in their pretty faces and slinky figures, and lavishing the sort of gifts on them that go with it.

For this you need to be well off really and lead a sort of Country Club life, which is not without its attendant risks and jealous moments, but presumably worth it.

Nora displayed no ambition to be like she was in her post school years, and was, in fact, rather self-satisfied and unenterprising it seemed to me.

Only a day or two before, I recalled, sliding unobtrusively into my corner of the office and letting my eyes rove over our executive secretary, Amanda Maddox only one year junior to Nora, I had tackled Nora about her drab appearance.

'Why don't you try and choose some clothes that will show off your good points more, and do your hair like you used to?' I had said, perhaps too pleadingly.

'Well I like to be comfortable and don't have to be smart like you for the office, and I'd sooner get on with my painting' - Nora does make a bit of a mess with oils and so on - 'and keeping the place clean than dress up,' was her reply.

This was Nora's usual response to what I regarded as my effort to encourage her, with a bit of a hint built into it that I thought she was letting herself go. Sometimes I got a nasty rejoinder.

Why aren't I content to be a man's man like a lot of my friends who seem to delight in a wife who cooks, keeps a more than tidy home and still socializes enough, I ask myself. Instead I can't help wanting mine to be a reflection of my own romanticism.

I do think that names affect people when they grow up, or, in the case of boys, earlier. I remember a boy at my school. His parents, thoughtlessly, but no doubt for their own reasons, had given him the name Marmaduke and he had a very bad time being ragged about it to begin with. Then he grew big and husky and started to assert himself. He then got called 'Duke' and he went from strength to strength, finishing up as head boy.

It was worth trying the idea on Nora, I decided.

Strangely my chance came quite soon, and when I got home one evening I said 'Nora, we got some models photographed to-day to advertise our products. One was called Leonora, what a smasher, and she actually looked a bit like you! I'm going to call you that.'

'Good heavens no,' said Nora, but I thought I spotted a responsive light in her eye. 'I mean what about our families and friends, Jack?'

'Well, it's not much of a changeover for them to make and if they stick to Nora for a time never mind. You can say it's good for your Art. Makes a good signature. We'll get used to it and so will they, and we will go on having new friends and connections.'

Nora softened visibly. 'I think I agree,' she said.

That was a year ago. You should see Leonora now. She is a corollary of her younger self, poised, svelte and popular. She has sold quite a few pictures, and as she has made a hit with my business associates, I'm doing all right too.

The Driving Test

by

Hazel Jackson

I've been going to take my driving test for as long as I can remember. Well, ever since Roger and I got married and we've just had our sixteenth wedding anniversary; not that we did anything special for it. I mean, Roger was working late and I was tired after my driving lesson anyway. Funny that I should have a lesson on that day. It should, in fact, have been my driving test but I cancelled it again. I know I shouldn't have, and everybody groaned about it, but I know that I'm still not ready. Anyway, I'm jumping ahead a bit. As I said I've been having driving lessons for sixteen years! What a laugh, you'd think I'd have given up by now, but not me. I'm quite a determined lady you see.

It was after we'd got married, as I said Roger had to work pretty hard in those days, mind you, he's always been a hard working chap. He's into computers, - they're his life really, absolutely besotted with them he is. Anyway, I found that I wasn't getting out much and I thought that if I learnt to drive I'd do a lot more. I'd been to evening classes mind you. I'm creative you see, so I need to release my ideas. I did art and sculpture to begin with. Brilliant fun it was, and me and the lads had a great time. It was mostly men in the class, I don't know why. Not that I minded because I always seem to get on better with men. Nothing naughty, you understand, I've always been true to Rog, it's just that men seem to understand me better. We used to have a few drinks after class and then they'd all cheer me off - because I was on my bike then as I couldn't drive. Yes, we had a real laugh in those days. Anyway, Rog was busy with his computers and I was feeling restricted, which isn't good if you're artistic.

Well, then Rog was moved to London. Big computer firm and he had to set it all up. He's a whizz at that kind of thing. So he was commuting and was usually shattered when he got home. That's when I had my first lessons. I've always had two a week. Tuesdays and Thursday's. Kind of splits the week up a bit. My first instructor was called Mike. We had such a laugh. Used to go all over the place we did. Driving around country villages - up to the common. We got to enjoy it so much that I started bringing a picnic after a while. He was married, but then it was all strictly above board of course. We used to spend more time on our picnics than we did on driving lesson's. Still, we had great fun, and you can't learn to drive unless you're pretty relaxed with you're instructor.

It was a real shame the way it ended though. People on our estate are so narrow minded you see. We were totally innocent, but of course the rumours started flying. Some people just can't bear to see others having good fun, can they? Mike's wife even phoned me up once. Gave me an absolute mouthful, of all the nerve. I told her straight that it was all completely untrue. We were just good friends and he was doing a great job teaching me to drive. I was getting on really well until then. Anyway, then Mike left the driving school and I was taken over by this stupid old idiot who was totally hopeless at teaching. And so serious. I just couldn't relax at all with him, so I stopped having lessons. I just wasn't getting anywhere. Rog didn't notice of course; he was involved with a new computer at that time and he gets totally one-track when he's got a new 'baby' as he calls it.

That was the next thing that stopped me taking the test, as it so happens. A baby. Funny really, I never thought I'd want children but along came Jodi. Sweet little thing she is, well not so little anymore of course. I still had lessons twice a week. Jodi used to be in the back in a carry-cot. What a laugh. You should have seen the instructors faces when I came out with her in my arms. Most of them thought I was too young to have a child. I've always had quite a youthful face you see and I keep myself quite slim. Anyway, we used to have quite a laugh with most of them but I couldn't concentrate well enough to take the test. Not with the baby in the back. I had some really sweet instructors though. I think I got quite a name at the driving schools. I knew every instructor in our area. A really sweet bunch. They'd all laugh and wave if I saw them when I was out shopping. Tuesdays and Thursdays. Its become my life really. Anyway, Jodi grew up and I became really determined to pass my test. The 'boys' as I called them even started laying bets on it. Cheeky lot. And I was all ready, feeling really confidant and then Rog came home one day and said we'd have to move because he'd been offered this brilliant computer job in Birmingham. He's the tops in computers you see. Absolutely rule his life they do.

Well that put paid to my test. I just went to pieces. My confidence went completely out the window.

So we moved. At least it got us away from that awful gossipy lot on the estate. Birmingham isn't too bad. We've got a nice house in a very select little cul-de-sac. I started evening classes again. Woodwork this time. It was a good group, mostly men of course. I didn't mind because I always get on well with men. Nothing funny of course. We even had a Christmas outing, we hired a mini-bus and went for a Chinese meal and then a disco. It was just me and the lads but what a time we had. I can't remember half of it I'm afraid. I don't usually drink you see and the Saki hit me for six! They said I was a little raver although I think they were just teasing me. Anyway, they got me back home and luckily Rog was asleep. He'd been working hard with his latest computers. He was doing ever so well at his new job. He's an absolute natural with computers. I don't know what he'd have thought if he'd seen me in that state, with all the wood working lads too. And it was all quite innocent.

That was ages ago now. I started driving lessons again just after that. At this new school, I got what I'd call 'an older man.' He always had a lovely aftershave on, I could smell it on my clothes for hours after the lesson. Beautiful soft hands he had and I'd always thought that men with gold chains were a bit vain, but not Derek. We didn't exactly have a laugh, he was too mature for that, but we had a rapport. Yes, a rapport. He used to come in for coffee after the lessons. We'd talk for ages about all sorts of things.

He left the school quite suddenly; he hadn't even said he was going. I heard later that he'd been having an affair with one of his pupils and that his wife had found out. He never mentioned to me that he was married. Anyway, I didn't believe a word of it. People can be so bitchy can't they. I'd almost felt ready for another try at the test before Derek left. It threw me completely though, especially with the nasty rumours.

I'm with Adrian now. Tuesday and Thursday's as usual, but I can't get on with him really. Nice lad, don't get me wrong, and lovely looking, but a bit effeminate. You know, limp-wristed. I'm not saying he 'is' mind you and anyway I think it's live and let live these days, but he's not my type - of instructor that is. Very sweet, but not my type. I think he's got a boyfriend, so my neighbour said. Nasty rumour to spread around I thought.

Anyway, I saw a very nice looking instructor the other day from a different school, so I thought I might change. Rog say's I should do another evening class. He's very busy at the moment you know, computers as usual. They're his life really. He's brilliant with them. So I think I might. Motor mechanics would be a good one, I could learn about the engine as well as the driving then. Do you know what one of my friends said the other day. (Well, she used to be a friend.) She said I should try a woman instructor. What a cheek. If I'd have thought a woman could teach me I'd have passed my test years ago. No, I shall just keep on trying. I am quite a determined lady you see. Do you know, I think I saw Mike the other day on the roundabout. I did wave and go round twice to try and catch his eye. Adrian nearly had a fit.

I don't think Mike saw me though. My very first instructor Mike was. Did I ever tell you about Mike? He was lovely!

A Taxi Driver's Tale

by

Llyn Morris

Before I start this little story I need to tell you that my family have lived in Mid-Wales and along the Border for - well, forever. What is more, most of them have earned their livings on the road - drovers, dealers, hauliers and such-like. I, too, earn my living on the road, for I am a taxi driver in Hereford.

One evening last October, after a day of pouring rain and miserable passengers, I'd just arrived home from work when a friend, Jim Lewis rang. Jim runs a parcels delivery business and I sometimes help him out when he has more work than he can cope with. That particular evening he had a parcel for a farm in the hills behind Hay-on-Wye. He asked me if I could run it up there because he had to take another one to Birmingham.

After a dismal day on the rank my eyeballs felt bruised and my neck was stiff with tension, but money's money after all, so I got out our family runabout, an old VW Golf, and - after a scene with the children, who clamoured to come, although it was far too late to take them - I collected the parcel and its documentation from Jim. What it contained is by-the-bye: I think it was animal medicines and it was addressed to a Mr R S Powell, Upper Hengwm Farm, a typical Welsh Border half-English, half-Welsh farm name.

Soon I was crossing that Border, John Dunn on the car radio, the rain easing off, stars starting to show above the silhouettes of the hills and all the tensions of my day starting to dissipate. I decided to stop for five minutes or so in Hay, to eat an apple which was rolling about in the glove compartment and to check on my map exactly where Upper Hengwm Farm was, although Jim (who'd delivered a parcel there once before) had said it was on the side of Hay Bluff.

No sooner had I stopped than I was kicking myself for a careless fool, for the map was nowhere in the car. Not to have your maps by you in my business is like being a surgeon without a scalpel. Too late did I remember that the children had helped me clean the interior of the Golf and that one of them had conscientiously put the maps on the kitchen window-sill while we were doing it - and we'd obviously forgotten to put them back!

However, I took the road up to the Bluff, as Jim had said I should. Right by the side of it was a farm with an outside light on. I saw the farmer latching his farm gate for the night and asked him the way. As up-country folks do, he knew Mr R S Powell as a neighbour, even though Upper Hengwm Farm was twenty minutes' drive away.

I found Mr Powell, his wife and three strapping sons in their slippers and at the tea-and-tv stage of the day when I knocked on their door. Powell Senior signed the receipt for the parcel and they gave me a cup of tea and a short account of how hard their lives were before I left.

It was probably because I was intent on the sports news that I took the wrong turning at the first road junction I came to, and I was a couple of miles along a mountain road before I realized I was driving deeper into Wales, not home to Hereford. Nor could I turn round, for the road was single-track, with no turning places and the mountainside below was precipitous. What was really infuriating was that away to my right I could see a mustardy glow in the sky, the reflection of the street lights of Hay.

Now, what happened next did not appear in the slightest bit strange to me at the time, although its eeriness haunts me as I write this account.

I arrived at an unsignposted fork in the road. Both of the roads at the fork were metalled, but the left-hand one seemed to lead deeper into Wales, whilst the right-hand road sloped down across the mountainside to where, about a quarter of a mile away, I could see a window-lit and - to my city eyes - an incredibly isolated cottage. Although I had never before been anywhere near this bit of country, I knew with perfect confidence that if I took this right-hand fork, past the cottage, it would lead me to a grassy drove-road which, in its turn, would take me to a metalled road lower down the mountain and then back to Hay.

The only two dangers, I knew, would be sliding over the edge of the drove-road and somersaulting down the mountainside, and that there would be a dip in the track, where a prill crossed it, and in which there would be a danger of getting stuck.

I switched off the car radio, the better to concentrate, and started down the right hand road. I crossed a clangorous cattle grid and glimpsed a figure which appeared in the cottage window - whoever it was no doubt wondering why on earth a VW Golf was descending a hill track on a wet autumn night.

I drove carefully in second gear, the dead bracken and bents shining unnaturally in the headlights. Rounding the shoulder of the mountain, I started to descend more sharply. I knew that I was approaching the prill and worried that I'd stick fast - although, to be honest, what was really worrying me was that, if I did get stuck, I'd be the laughing stock of my mates on the taxi rank for weeks.

I decided to yump the prill. I accelerated - still in second - keeping my hands loose on the steering-wheel, thumbs outside it, in case, in reaction to banging a rut or a stone, I should over twist the wheel and overturn the car. My headlights caught a small bunch of rushes and a vein of water. I jabbed my right foot down; I felt the front wheels flute and spin - my heart punched away in fear - then they gripped and I shot away.

I topped a little ridge and took a few deep breaths to dispel the breathlessness of fear. It was, I knew, downhill all the way from now on, literally and figuratively. I would follow the track until I reached a newly pleached hedge, which was the boundary of the highest field enclosed from the mountain. The track would run along the top side of this hedge and, at the corner of the field, where grew three or four crab apple trees, I would pick up the Hay road.

There's little more to say. I reached the hedge but was faintly disappointed to find it overgrown, although I could see in my headlights the old pleachers rotting in its bottom. Nor were there any crab apple trees. Instead there was an old railway van in which a farmer probably stored some fodder for outlying cattle. Nevertheless, when - with, I admit, relief - I turned onto the metalled road, I noticed behind the van a wind blasted skeleton of what might have been a crab apple tree.

I returned to Hay, then Hereford and home. Here my story ends, although - let me repeat - I swear I had never been near that fork in the road, that cottage, before; nor have I been there since. I swear I had no qualms whatsoever about descending that drove road that night. Only now, writing this account in my armchair, do I feel an eerie sense of the Past swirling around my familiar sitting room like the mist you meet on the road just before dawn.

Gulf

by

Amanda Corner

We knew we had to remember this moment; like people know where they were when JFK was shot. They talk about things like that on the radio. I remember a woman saying she was under the table when she heard Kennedy was dead. Or maybe I've remembered that wrong; but we were sat around a table, a drunken curry, about midnight. Opposite one man was slumped asleep over the table and next to him another sat bolt upright, mouth open, eyes closed. A woman walked in, she said

'It's started. The Americans have gone in.' We all looked at each other. Some said it was sad. Some said it was great. Some said let's get it over with fast.

The American woman with us was pregnant. Her friends were bombing Baghdad and inside her child was creating itself, becoming more and more complex, moment by moment adding cells, growing layers of skin, eyelashes, toes. I asked her if she was glad she was pregnant, she said yes, but perhaps not now.

On the radio they give us the latest on the Gulf War. Then it's 'Now we go over to Gardener's Question Time.' On television we get a brief respite from 'Neighbours.'

I go shopping down the High street. I don't know if the people serving me are Pakistani, Iranian or Iraqi. I don't know how to speak to them anymore. The ground beneath me has shifted. We hear planes going over early in the morning. I buy a tray to stop my tea dripping on your floor. I buy a nice black and white striped one. It costs one pound fifty. It seems silly to be buying a tray this morning. I feel as if it might be the end of the world and I wonder how much use I'll get out of it. I try to think about practical things, like I need a job and I must get some ground coffee, some cigarettes. But it doesn't really work. I don't know what to feel.

Yesterday I bled for the first time in nearly two years. Ha, it seems as if I was bleeding with the soldiers. I changed back into a woman. Was it the man who has just come back into my life that turned me into a woman? Do I suddenly need to be a woman again after all this time? What was it that told my body that it needed to bleed?

I was in a taxi on my way to meet him. The driver said it was late to be going out. As he said this we passed Kings Cross station. I thought he might think I was a prostitute so I had to explain and it was hard for me to say 'Boyfriend', 'My Boyfriend.'

'I'm going to meet my boyfriend in the pub.' I haven't used a sentence like that for seven years, so I felt as if I was lying.

We live in this flat and we stay five feet apart, except for special occasions. I try hard not to make it matter. I try so hard that my concentration makes me silent. I hope I'm not losing myself. I suppose I just have to accept that you want me to be here even if you don't show it very much. I will try to remember this always.

A siren. A child screams *'Mummy'*. I freeze. Is it on the television or coming from outside? Am I supposed to be scared? Nothing is certain and I have lost my previous routine. Last week I knew where I was. I stood in a restaurant, I served people, I smiled, I knew these people. And I was coming here to you. You had asked me to come here. Now I am surrounded by people I don't know, people I must get to know. And not being known I sometimes don't know who I am. I wish my friends would ring me up; I need something familiar again. I think of the soldiers in the desert trying to become familiar with a foreign land; learning to differentiate between one sand mound and another. Now they know where they stand. It's a red alert and they're allowed to act.

You go out and you come back. I don't always want to be here when you come back but I don't know where to go. I've forgotten how difficult these things can be. When I go out the men hang out of their windows and whistle at me. In the street people follow me; they say things. I kept thinking the taximan wouldn't take me to where I wanted to go. If he didn't take me to you how would you know where to find me? He was a nice man but I couldn't be sure until he had delivered me safely. We talked about the War as we drove through Camden, but it hadn't started then. He was worried about his job because petrol would go up to four pounds a gallon, he'd heard. From now on when you don't give me what I want I shall go and flirt with the boys in the fruit and veg shop.

I don't dare put the radio on because of the war. Its turned into the latest and greatest Soap Opera. Suddenly everything has the ability to affect my mood. I am horribly open. I used to be cast in iron. I was always on the level. Now there's such a crashing crushing me. It comes from all angles and I don't even know what it is. I must build myself back up again and tuck in all the nerves. I need something really frivolous now, like to watch Top of the Pops.

In the restaurant he said 'Fuck the war, let's get back to Glamour.' This morning I read the origins of the word 'Glamour', it was all to do with witches and the threat and fear of the feminine. But the threat now is all male. I wonder if I can bear to watch another episode of 'The Gulf War'. I have been sitting in silence because the words hurt my ears. I know it's going on but if I don't see it I can pretend it's an ordinary, everyday Thursday. And tomorrow it's Friday and I shall watch a different screen, it will be a nice film and things will be nice again.

It was nice on Tuesday. I sat listening to Erik Satie. There were lights on in the building opposite. People moved, one, two three, from cupboard to sink. I was happy to be in here, not there. I watched the black Plane tree merging with the sky, growing darker, deep blue to black in just the few moments that I sat there, looking out. A red jumper. A big, red back in the window opposite. A big red back throwing red tea towels around the room. But even then I was thinking that war may break out soon. But families have to be fed and so women in red jumpers go on cooking. 5.15pm and everyone is waiting. For rice to soften, potatoes to roast, people to return, war to begin. It was all so still, no breeze, just the cold air turning the pavements white.

Rivers of blood, now that's all I can think of. And it's such a long day. The television still says 'The Gulf War Day One' I think of the blood of the soldiers, the blood of me, the blood lining the American woman's womb. Her blood cushions and protects the foetus inside her but the blood that seeps from the soldiers is their lifeline leaving them; it is their death coming out. This calms me for some reason, perhaps because I am familiar with blood where I am not familiar with rockets.

And now we have our own Gulf War in this flat. Negotiations, as they say, have broken down. Whereas yesterday when you came home you came straight to me, today you hesitate. You spend a long time getting out of your coat and scarf, you fiddle with the fire, the curtains, then turn to me and smile, sort of. Awkward. Very awkward. And awkwardly I sit taking all this in; my back to the typewriter, just watching you, unaware of whether you are aware of me watching you.

The silence is building walls around us. It is probably too late to save whatever it was we briefly had. It seems it would be ridiculous to try. I daren't even mention the words *you, me, relationship,* they would startle you now. I feel as if I dreamt it all up and made you, against your will, act it all out with me. I don't know where you've been when you've been here with me, but now it seems like you weren't here at all.

I was in a taxi on my way to meet him. The driver said it was late to be going out. As he said this we passed Kings Cross station. I thought he might think I was a prostitute so I had to explain and it was hard for me to say 'Boyfriend', 'My Boyfriend.'

'I'm going to meet my boyfriend in the pub.' I haven't used a sentence like that for seven years, so I felt as if I was lying.

We live in this flat and we stay five feet apart, except for special occasions. I try hard not to make it matter. I try so hard that my concentration makes me silent. I hope I'm not losing myself. I suppose I just have to accept that you want me to be here even if you don't show it very much. I will try to remember this always.

A siren. A child screams 'Mummy'. I freeze. Is it on the television or coming from outside? Am I supposed to be scared? Nothing is certain and I have lost my previous routine. Last week I knew where I was. I stood in a restaurant, I served people, I smiled, I knew these people. And I was coming here to you. You had asked me to come here. Now I am surrounded by people I don't know, people I must get to know. And not being known I sometimes don't know who I am. I wish my friends would ring me up; I need something familiar again. I think of the soldiers in the desert trying to become familiar with a foreign land; learning to differentiate between one sand mound and another. Now they know where they stand. It's a red alert and they're allowed to act.

You go out and you come back. I don't always want to be here when you come back but I don't know where to go. I've forgotten how difficult these things can be. When I go out the men hang out of their windows and whistle at me. In the street people follow me; they say things. I kept thinking the taximan wouldn't take me to where I wanted to go. If he didn't take me to you how would you know where to find me? He was a nice man but I couldn't be sure until he had delivered me safely. We talked about the War as we drove through Camden, but it hadn't started then. He was worried about his job because petrol would go up to four pounds a gallon, he'd heard. From now on when you don't give me what I want I shall go and flirt with the boys in the fruit and veg shop.

I don't dare put the radio on because of the war. Its turned into the latest and greatest Soap Opera. Suddenly everything has the ability to affect my mood. I am horribly open. I used to be cast in iron. I was always on the level. Now there's such a crashing crushing me. It comes from all angles and I don't even know what it is. I must build myself back up again and tuck in all the nerves. I need something really frivolous now, like to watch Top of the Pops.

140

Love and Let Love

by

Marie Nicholls

She slumped forward in her chair, rocking herself, her arms tightly clasped around her breasts and her head pressed low to one side so that her cheek seemed to caress her own naked shoulder as her silk dressing gown, unbelted, had slipped open and hung untidy and disregarded, revealing her middle aged and overweight body. Her face was bloated and patched red from crying and an occasional deep sob, terrible in the way it seemed to tear her very soul from her, racked her whole body. Her old dog stood beside her, anxiously watching her and giving the occasional nudge to her arm with his cracked, dry old nose, a movement which normally provoked at least a small caress to his silky head, but which today went completely unnoticed. The telephone sat there on the stained coffee table, hard, unmoving, shining forth its cheery innocence, oblivious of having just been the means of delivering her death sentence. Not quick, mortal death, which at this moment she would embrace gladly; but the lingering death of loneliness, of being unwanted. There was no-one she could turn to, no-one in the world on whom she could unload some of her misery.

Frustration, anger at her own stupidity, began to mingle with her self-pitying pain and gave a kind of strength to her devastated body. Shuddering, she drew a deep breath and slowly stood up, laying a hand lovingly on her dog's head as she did so. Pulling her gown close around her and re-tying the peach coloured sash, she went into her bedroom where she pulled open the bottom drawer of her dressing table and drew out from under an untidy pile of underwear a sheaf of papers of different shapes and sizes, mostly bearing messages of a few words. Her eyes rested listlessly on the topmost message: 'Called at six pm. Where were you? Will call at eight. *Don't ring!*' Sitting on the edge of the bed she looked through the papers, reminding herself for how long she'd longed to end this one-sided relationship, in which she'd just had to wait to receive whatever he chose to give her and whenever he chose to give it. It wasn't just the knowledge that she was 'the other woman' who was prepared to risk hurting a woman who'd never done her any harm. Strangely enough she didn't really care very much about that. She'd often wondered about her lack of guilt feelings, when, God knew, she'd felt guilty most of her life without doing anything very wrong at all! It wasn't even the knowledge that he made love to his wife two or three times a week in most imaginative ways. After all, she had nothing to complain about there, since they'd made love almost every day for the last three years. No. What made her angry with herself was the way she accepted from him treatment that no-one else in the world would dare to offer her. He shouted her down when she tried to put her point of view and he'd accused her unjustly of flirting with other men. He was vulgar and cruel in his judgment of other women. He spied on her even to the extent of peering through her windows or entering the house and evesdropping when she'd had friends calling. Eventually she'd stopped everyone from visiting and sealed her own fate of loneliness.

A thin and bitter smile twisted her red, bloated face as she gazed at herself in the mirror. He'd been the man of her dreams, remember? The man who'd re-awoken love in her heart which had become barren after years of begging for physical love from a husband who screwed his and everybody else's secretary but wouldn't screw her. How she'd begged him to touch her breasts or stroke her belly! How she wondered what he was like with his mistresses and why he wanted them and refused her! For years she'd believed herself to be undesirable, had crushed her own sexuality, finding that the occasional desperate foray into infidelity only heightened her awareness of her deprivation. And then, when she'd gone through all the anguish of divorce and tried to start her life anew, what was the first thing she did but got involved with this bastard, not only a married man with three sons, not only a complete and utter unbalanced sex maniac, but a priest to cap it all!

And now he'd rung to say he'd never see her again, that it was all over - after the three years she'd given to him - because he was convinced that she'd had another man in the house overnight when in fact there wasn't even a man there, just an old girlfriend and her baby. The thinking side of her brain told her she should shout 'three cheers' and welcome the break which it craved; but the part of her that had been starved for so long mourned, weeping for the death of excitement, of passion, of at least the pretence that she had something precious to offer and that her body was desirable.

Again the wry smile as she looked in the mirror. Desirable? That? Yet she knew she *did* have something to give, that she was a good lover, even if only because she was prepared to give everything, do anything to give pleasure, to be appreciated. She saw stretching ahead of her days even worse than the days of waiting that lay behind her. At least those days had culminated in hours of sex, hours when he had shouted out words of love, hours when her body, her face, her mouth, had experienced passion and desire, had tasted joy at least of a kind. The renewed realisation of her loss swept over her and the painful tears began to flow again as her crumpled body let the lassitude of sorrow bear down on her. Sleep came over her all unknowing.

She awoke in the early hours, cold and stiff, her head acheing and her eyes swollen and sore. She picked up the papers that lay strewn around her and read their messages: *Back at six. Wear the black leather.' 'Pick me up at four. She's going to be out for a couple of hours.' 'Where were you at midnight? You didn't answer the phone!'* She remembered those phone calls, checking up on her, day and night, while she, of course, could not ring his house in case his wife answered the phone. She, who was honest to him, loyal to him, who had at first really loved him, was hounded and accused yet went on trying to believe in her own loving, all the time knowing what a bastard the man was. She knew he'd had plenty of other lovers, that she wasn't the only one even now, yet she'd let him go on shitting on her even till now. For what? For the dubious pleasure of a few orgasms while being used to satisfy a perverted man's lust? She knew that even the words of love he used to her were partly to keep her quiet, partly because he knew that they pleased her, made her come more easily and so increased his own sense of power. But when he was lying with her, when he stroked her face and called her his beautiful lover, reality was suspended; she chose to believe she was indeed desired and loved - though she was always afterwards to be hurt by the barbs of truth as they bit into her sensible consciousness.

She looked down again at the papers she'd gathered in her hand, placed then on the bed beside her and rummaged in the still open drawer, pulling out a white plastic vicar's 'dog collar' that he'd forgotten to replace one day. These scraps were her only tools for revenge. She told herself that this wasn't just going to be revenge for herself alone. He must have hurt so many women in his time and no doubt would take advantage of many more if given free rein. The man was a fiend and had to be stopped.

She lay back on the bed and let her mind recall the way it had all begun; how he had called on her every day when she moved here alone, unsure and broken; how he had made her feel like a real woman, beautiful even; how he had eventually made love to her in ways she had never even dreamed of so that she knew passion and joy and the complete satisfaction of her own womanhood.

145

Abruptly, she thrust all these fragments of her recent past back into the drawer and gathering her long greying hair into a knot went to the bathroom to wash and prepare for what she believed would be the first day of the rest of her life.

Time To Change

by

Deborah Thompson

Deb was fed up with her job. It had got to the stage where she did not even want to get up in the morning. The job was supposed to be a good one, she was well paid and held a fairly responsible position, but it felt so wrong. For years she had studied and worked to get a job like this and now found that it was worthless. The worst thing was that she could not leave, how could she pay her half of the mortgage if she did?

The other half, mortgage payer and partner, did not want her to leave. It was a very selfish thing for Deb to think of doing. He was struggling to set up his own business, with all the pressures that involved, and did not want the added pressure of becoming the sole breadwinner. So they argued, him exasperated by her willingness to throw away their security, her increasingly frustrated by work and his lack of support.

Every day she came home wound up and ready to snap at the slightest provocation. He was becoming the enemy, he would not let her stop working, he wanted her to carry on in this intolerable situation. Deb resented him for it. She was getting very difficult to live with, he could not understand it. He only wanted her to wait, to hang on until he was sure he could manage it on his own. She felt as though she had waited too long already, life was too short to throw away like this. The mortgage hung over them like a guillotine.

One Tuesday morning she got up, late as usual, and dressed quickly. She rushed out of the house, the beautiful house that she never had time to appreciate. She longed to stay, sit on the comfy chair and stare out of the window, just relaxing and enjoying the view. Instead she rushed away in her company car to the office. The car was another useless perk, only really used for going to work. It would be better to walk than to work in hell. The journey went as usual, completed in a daydream, until the dreaded building came into view. She had a strong urge to drive away, turn back and go home. Again she suppressed the urge and drove into the car park.

Once inside it was back to the boring office routine, she had being doing it for years now. Each new project was harder than the last one, not to do but to want to do. Currently she was supposed to be learning the most boring computer language ever invented. It was so tedious, so meaningless, she could hardly bear pretending to do it properly. Deb whiled away the morning daydreaming and trying to memorise parts of the language. Occasionally she got to talk to a colleague, just small talk, but it was a break. Mostly she thought about leaving, having time to think and do something positive, instead of slowly rotting. Was choosing the wrong job a mistake that lasted for life? Was it a trap?

At lunchtime she headed home again. Neal would have cooked lunch for her, as he worked from home. As she drove she saw the river, the road went right down to the bank. She thought about the possible escape, driving in. No more work, no more arguments, an end to frustration. Her end. The pain would go, but so would everything else. It was not the right solution, she knew if she could just leave her job things would get better.

A huge argument followed when she got home, they would never agree on this. Something had to give, either Debs sanity or her job. Her life or her love. Neal stormed out of the house, he was furious with her. She was not only foolish and irresponsible, she was selfish and miserable too.

Deb sat alone in their house. Her mind was racing, searching for a way out of the mess. Leave work and lose her home and the most important person in her life. Wait until she found something else to do, where she could still pay her way. But waiting any longer would mean more desperation, more misery and more chance of destroying their relationship. Whatever she did would be wrong. In the end her survival instinct told her she must hand in her notice, to preserve her sanity. Her life and happiness had to be the prime considerations, without these there was nothing, and with them there was a chance. A chance to start again, be happy, make him happy. She had to do it. She left him a note, explaining that she was handing in her notice and why. Telling him that she knew he might leave her, but if she stayed at work she was sure he would leave her.

Back at work she wrote out and handed in her notice with great relief at last. People seemed surprised, they must not have realised how she felt. There was light at the end of the tunnel now, she had hope for the future.

The phone on her desk rang, she answered, 'Extension 141.'

Neal spoke, 'Hello.'

She felt terrible, he must have read the note and phoned to shout at her. 'Hello.' She replied.

'How are you?' he asked,

'I'm fine.' She waited for his angry reprimands.

'I've been looking for those glasses you wanted, but the shop was shut,' Neal said, without a hint of anger. It gradually dawned on her, he was phoning to make up after their argument and he had not read the note.

'Haven't you seen my note?'

'What note?'

'On the table, I think you'd better read it.'

It was quiet for a minute as he read the note, the time passed so slowly as she waited to see what he would say.

'Have you done it?' He finally asked.

'Yes, I'm sorry I had to. I hope you won't leave me.' Her future hung in the air, waiting for his answer.

'Don't be silly, of course I won't leave you Deb, we'll manage.'

She started to cry, a real miracle, as they were tears of happiness, something she never dreamed would happen whilst sat in her office prison. At that moment she knew that she had done the right thing and life was going to be good from now on. More importantly whatever happened she knew that they would manage.

A Clean Bill Of Health

by

Yvonne Thomas

Facing a major operation is a traumatic experience, as anyone in the same circumstances will confirm, but with Mabel by my side, I felt better able to cope with the situation. Her soothing words seemed to relax and comfort me. Dear Mabel, she had proved such a wonderful friend. When no-one else seemed interested in me, Mabel befriended me and showed me affection I had never experienced before.

Like me, she was getting on in years, and perhaps that was why she seemed to understand me. We had certainly enjoyed some marvellous times together. Our little trips to town, jaunts to the countryside and even excursions to the coast. I had never seen the sand and sea before. It was all a new and wonderful experience to me.

I even accompanied Mabel to her grand-daughter's wedding. Not that her daughter had been very keen on the idea Mabel had confided to me later, but she had insisted. I felt very smart, dressed up in all my finery especially for the occasion. It was a touching picture.... the bride in her beautiful long, white lace dress, and I'll never forget those sweet little bridesmaids in their pale pink dresses and carrying baskets of pink rose-buds. Mabel cried! I broke down too, and all Mabel's daughter kept saying was,

'I told you not to bring her Mum. I knew she would show you up and be an embarrassment to you.'

Me, an embarrassment! What a wicked and unkind comment to make!

I was relieved to know that Mabel wasn't cross with me. As always, she understood that my problems were mainly due to old age and being ill-treated in earlier life. However, it certainly made her view me in a different light, and from that day onwards, her face wore a worried frown as she showed great concern about my condition. My continual coughing and trembling after the experience at the wedding, seemed to worry her even more, and eventually, she insisted that I go for a check up. I was frightened about that, but Mabel's soothing words had put me at ease, and I survived the examination with few problems. However, it was decided that a major operation was necessary, and that's what I now had to face.

150

Those big buildings have a certain smell about them that's enough to make you pass out on entering them. I was grateful to Mabel for being there, but she could only stay with me for so long........... after that I was on my own!

The waiting made it so unbearable. Having come this far, I just wanted to get it over and done with. I flinched as the team of experienced white coated men approached me, but I managed to grin and bear it when they probed inside me with those shining silver tools. Within a few hours, it was all over, and I was relieved to see Mabel by my side, and to hear the words, 'We're happy to report a clean bill of health. She'll be O.K. for a few more miles now that we've changed her engine and done the M.O.T.'

Bitter Conflict

by

Joy Jarvis

Ann Forester sat in front of the fire, chin in cupped hand, moodily looking into its flickering flames. The only sound in the room was the ticking of a grandfather clock standing against one of the walls.

It was a room which displayed its owner's taste. It matched her elegant appearance which was only marred by the loose white cotton gloves she was wearing.

Ann sighed as she held out her hands; then grimaced at the sight of them sheathed in their ugly covering. The greasy medication prescribed by the doctor for the flaking skin had been useless, but she had to persevere with the treatment - after all there was nothing else she could do.

Harry, her husband, rarely concerned himself about her. He was out with his so called friends leaving her alone as usual. What had gone wrong with their marriage? She shrugged her shoulders. She knew the answer only too well. She was in her forties when she had married him and, as a fairly wealthy widow, she should have known what had appealed to him! He had not bothered to keep a job since their marriage; the last one had been selling life insurance. That had bored him after a few weeks. He had since been at a loose end, and had become more difficult to live with.

She had met Harry while on holiday alone in the south of France. The constant attention of a good looking young man had weakened her usual good judgement. She had not hesitated when within a month of their meeting he had asked her to marry him.

Harry had been such a contrast to her first husband. James had been elderly and ailing. She had nursed him for years until his death.

Ann asked herself, as she had done so many times recently, why did she stay with Harry? There was absolutely nothing to prevent her leaving him. Was she so dependent physically on him? When he was in the mood, he was a good lover, but, surely that was not enough.

She wondered what he had meant last night when he had suddenly shouted at her that it would all end soon. The clock chimed - ten o' clock; Ann heard the front door open and then being slammed shut. She rose from her chair and walked out into the hall.

Harry had his back to her as he hung his overcoat in the small cloakroom to the left of the door. He turned and saw her standing at the foot of the stairs.

'So my loving wife has been waiting up for me.'

Ann flinched at his sarcastic tone.

'You needn't have bothered. The sight of you forever scratching your hands drives me up the wall. Look, you're scratching them now.'

Ann ascended the stairs. She paused when Harry called her.

'Ann, I'm sorry. Please come down. I want to talk to you.'

Ann turned to face him. 'No Harry. I'm going to bed. You can talk to me in the morning.'

'Ann, I want to talk to you now. I've got something important to tell you.'

'What is it that's so important it can't wait until the morning?'

'Come closer, Ann,' he invited.

Ann hesitated before moving nearer. Harry put an arm around her shoulders, lightly at first; then, as he started to speak, he tightened his grip.

'Remember I told you last night I'd find a way to end it all?' His voice dropped almost to a whisper. From his pocket he took out something which glinted in the light.

'This gun will do just that. It's small, but quite lethal at close range.'

With a cry Ann twisted away from Harry's grip and stepped backwards. 'Don't be a fool, Harry. Put that gun away, or give it to me.'

'You want it, you come and get it,' he answered.

Ann, with growing horror, realised that Harry was deliberately stage managing the situation. This scene was to end in an 'accident' with herself as the victim.

She looked towards the telephone and moved forward, but Harry stepped in front of it. Fear made Ann lunge at him. This time she managed to grab the hand holding the gun, but the white gloves made it difficult for her to hold on. They struggled for a few minutes; then the gun discharged. Ann felt Harry's grip on her slackening. His eyes changed swiftly from an angry glare to a look of disbelief. He sank slowly to the floor. Blood seeped through the front of his shirt.

After staring at Harry's body lying on the floor for some time, Ann went to the telephone, dialled 999 and asked for the police. Quite calmly she gave her name and address and said there had been a shooting accident.

Soon she heard a car pulling up outside. She opened the door and let in a police constable. After a brief glance at the scene he hurried back to his car. Using the radio he reported what he had found.

Later as Ann paced up and down her bedroom floor she could hear various sounds from below - men moving about, voices and, eventually, the sound of an ambulance arriving to take her husband's body away.

When an inspector arrived to take charge Ann told him the whole story, omitting nothing that had happened from the time her husband had arrived home.

'It was an accident,' she told him. Had he believed her, she wondered. He had left her after asking some questions, and now she could only wait while the investigations continued.

All the events of the night crowded in on her. She dropped into a chair, hands thrust deeply into her pockets. In answer to a tap on the door she called, 'Come in.'

It was the police inspector.

'I'm sorry to trouble you again, Mrs Forester. I know you must be feeling tired. There are, however, just a few more questions I must ask you.'

'You had better sit down, Inspector,' Ann said. He did so.

'I've had a few words with your next door neighbours, Mrs Forester. They said they heard your husband arriving home and, later, the sounds of a quarrel, which corroborates your story. They also added that this was not the first time they had heard you quarrelling.'

Ann admitted there had been quarrels which had occurred more frequently of late. Her husband had spent a great deal of time with his friends, leaving her alone. When she remonstrated with him he had always become very angry, but he had never threatened her before tonight. She had not even known that he owned a gun.

'I've already told you, Inspector, that I thought Harry was deliberately trying to create a situation in which there was to be an accident.'

'Yes, you have indeed, Mrs Forester.'

'By the way,' he went on quietly,' we found the telephone receiver dangling from the hall-table. Did you not replace it after calling us?'

'I don't know,' Ann replied. 'I don't remember what happened after I used the 'phone.'

Still in a quiet voice the inspector said gravely. 'Routine testing of the 'phone has revealed only one set of prints on it, and they are your husband's. That is rather strange, Mrs Forester. I suggest that it was in fact you who first produced

154

the gun and it was your husband who tried to use the telephone to call for help. Obviously, if that was the case your prints would not be on the instrument.'

Ann shook her head. 'All that I have told you is true,' she insisted. 'The fact that there are no fingerprints of mine on the telephone bears out what I say because,' she paused; then slowly took her hands out of her pockets and showed them to the inspector.

'Skin trouble,' she explained briefly. 'I've been wearing these cotton gloves day and night for weeks because of the medication I've had to use.'

Before the police left they told her she would be advised the date of the inquest.

The next morning Ann drew back the curtains. The sun was shining. She smiled. Now she was free again. Soon she would sell this awful house; then she chuckled as she remembered something. What a good idea of Harry's to take out those substantial life insurance policies on each other!